JOURNEY
FOR
JOEDEL

By Guy Owen

Fiction
Season of Fear
The Ballad of the Flim-Flam Man
Journey for Joedel

Poetry
Cape Fear Country and Other Poems
The White Stallion

Criticism
Essays in Modern American Literature (Co-editor)
Modern American Poetry: Essays in Criticism (Editor)

JOURNEY FOR JOEDEL

A
NOVEL
BY
GUY OWEN

CROWN PUBLISHERS, INC., NEW YORK

COPYRIGHT © 1970 BY GUY OWEN
LIBRARY OF CONGRESS CATALOG CARD NUMBER: 73-108076
MANUFACTURED IN THE UNITED STATES OF AMERICA
PUBLISHED SIMULTANEOUSLY IN CANADA BY
GENERAL PUBLISHING COMPANY LIMITED

Designed by Iris Kleinman

To my sons, James and Leslie, for whom I am well traded

JOURNEY
FOR
JOEDEL

I

WHEN THE ROOSTER SPLINTERED THE MIDNIGHT
air, the boy sleeping under the open barn shelter awoke. He
slept on the ground on a patchwork quilt, his right arm flung
out far enough to catch the dew in his palm. He was tall and
gangly for thirteen, his hair black and coarse, and in the weak
lantern light his lean face was dark-shadowed and coppery. His
body sprang alert, fully dressed except for shoes, tense with the
promise of the new day and the journey awaiting, for this was
opening day at the Clayton tobacco market.

With the bantam's premature cry, Joedel (short for Joe
Dell) twisted to one elbow, watching his father's tall form on
the board tossed over two sawhorses near the door. His mother
and sister were asleep in the rusty bed at the other end of the
barn, away from the heat and crackle of the brick furnace. Ever
since their well had been poisoned with kerosene, they were
afraid to sleep in the tenant house alone during the tobacco
curing.

The boy arose and checked the thermometer. To save
oil, his father had turned the lantern wick too low, and he
had to squint sleepily in order to read the temperature.

9

Clinton Shaw grunted, brushing a moth from his white face. "What's it read?" He had not been asleep. He took a special pride in his curing, and he rarely dozed on the uncomfortable board, as if he were cooking cane syrup instead of curing tobacco.

"It's right at two hundred, Papa," the boy whispered so as not to wake the others.

"Throw in one of them pine logs. We might finish her off before we leave." His father did not lower his voice, and it echoed back from the house and outbuildings in the warm darkness, scaring up a night bird.

The slender boy heaved the resinous pine wood into the furnace and clanged the iron door shut. Restless, he walked barefooted to the far end of the shelter, wiping the sticky sap on his overalls. He stood by the iron bed, where the tobacco sticks leaned neatly against the log wall. By the bed were an old Sears catalogue and a ball of knotted, used twine the size of a cantaloupe. He looked toward the packhouse and barn lot, then at his sleeping mother under the rough sack sheet. Her face was the color of a crawfish, her body swollen hugely with child. His baby sister gritted her teeth, one arm around Maddie, her dark hair spilling off the pillow tick like black molasses, almost touching her corn-shuck doll on the ground. The boy picked a firefly off her tar-black hair and gently threw it over the stringer, watching it light up in the darkness. He wished dawn would hurry up and come.

"You'd best get your sleep out," his father said, his voice gruff on the night air.

Joedel lay down again, staring out at the stars that were like bits of mica on velvet. For a long while he could not surrender to sleep again. Instead he lay on the hard earth sorting out the sounds of the warm August night, the cry of crickets and rainfrogs beyond the dry crackle of flames in the furnace. He was too full of the special day to sleep again, he thought, so there was nothing to do but lie awake waiting for Mr. Jim Eller's shrill whistle from the Big House on the hill.

Around him flowed the night sounds of the farm: Bessie's gentle bell as she stirred in her stall, and, near the house, the ghostly scrape of the catalpa tree as the thin breeze rose and fell. Once he heard the rattle of the hound dog's chain. The dog was tied to the chinaberry tree by his bedroom, guarding the tobacco that was graded and tied and pressed, ready to haul in the Hoover cart to the auction. Across the Cape Fear River he heard the diminishing cries of a pack of hounds chasing a fox.

Inside the barn the hot flues were popping again, as loud as small Chinese firecrackers. The staccato sound reminded him of hail on a tin roof, and the boy thought of the cruel storm that almost destroyed their crop and, more than that, his father's dream of buying some land of his own from Mr. Jim Eller at the end of the season.

The storm had blown up quickly that June afternoon. Joedel was feeding the dark-eyed coon in the wire cage beside the smokehouse and teasing his baby sister with some riddles. Clint Shaw was spraying the ten-inch tobacco plants, the heavy compressed-air tank strapped over his shoulder. After every four rows he walked to the barrel by the well, which his son kept full, his blue work shirt stained with a mixture of sweat and white poison.

"What goes to the water and never drinks?" Joedel asked Sissie.

"That's easy. A wagon."

"All right, then. What's red inside and full of little niggers?"

Sissie smiled. "I know that one. Grandma Oxendine told it to me. It's a muskmelon. No, wait a minute. It's a watermelon."

"You're a smart gal," the boy said, "but I'll bet you can't get this one:

"Round as a riddle,
Deep as a spring,
Been the death of many a pretty thing."

The answer was a gun, but he did not wait for an answer. Suddenly Joedel noticed that the white leghorns had become still, as though a hawk had shadowed the yard. Not a bird sang. Then his glance caught the greenish tinge to the clouds rolling eastward, as if following the Cape Fear River toward Wilmington and the sea. He had never seen such a shade of green in the sky, such ominous clouds.

Maddie was at the back door calling them in, the screen held open, and Clint Shaw had slipped the tank from his shoulder. He was running toward the barn, his field-tanned face contorted.

Then the murderous hail came down.

Joedel pulled Sissie under the plow shed by the crib, just as Clint lunged under it. The three of them stood speechless while the hail fell all around them. It made a deafening clatter on the old shingles. The stones were as large as chinaberries, then, finally, the size of bantam eggs, striking the earth with such force they bounced a foot off the ground. The boy observed how they seemed not to fall from the sky but appeared to squirt up from the earth, as if from the holes of night crawlers, falling back until the entire barnyard was covered with pretty white balls.

The strong wind twisted the chinaberry tree, and the deadly hail stripped away the leaves and green berries. Joedel watched the icy stones bounce off the three martin gourds over the garden fence, shredding his mother's rank sunflowers along the mesh wire. The old scarecrow, which wore his father's castoff overalls, seemed to buckle under the weight of the flailing hailstones, sagging in the stripped yellow corn.

Then as swiftly as it came, the storm blew over, and the sun came out, steaming the wet earth.

Sissie popped a large hailstone into her mouth, sucking until the ice melted.

Joedel dashed awkwardly about in the barnyard, picking up a handful of the largest stones. "Look, Papa. They're big as guinea eggs."

The two children followed Clint as he walked speechless

toward the tobacco field. Scampering behind him, they pelted each other with the quickly melting balls of ice. It was the first hailstorm Sissie had ever seen and she danced about squealing with delight.

"You younguns quit that horsing." It was their mother. She had walked from the house, where all the windows on the south side were broken. "It's nothing to kite around about." Her blue-black hair was drawn up in a severe bun, her coppery face grim. Her hands were clasped under her apron.

But the children had already become hushed. For there in the path were three dead biddies that had been caught by the hail. Their yellow fluff was beaten away and they lay pinkly naked in the crushed ragweed.

"Poor little biddies," Sissie said, her nose quivering like a rabbit's.

Then Joedel saw his father.

Clint Shaw had walked across the furrows toward the dropped tank, his face bleak. All around him the green leaves had been stripped from the stalks. As far as he could see there were only melting hailstones on the steamy earth and the riddled leaves of tobacco. His shadow lay shriveled at his feet.

"Clint?"

As Joedel watched, his father's shoulders slumped. The boy was reminded of the bent scarecrow in the ruined garden. Clint Shaw held his arms out, palms up, then let them fall by his side. Joedel had never seen his father's face so hurt, not even when their cow was foundered.

As she watched, Sissie spit out a ball of ice.

The June sun bore down on them and soon there were no more hailstones, only gummy leaves shredded on the plowed loam.

Their backs were to the road and they did not hear Mr. Eller's old Studebaker drive up. But directly he was striding up the ruined rows, his short legs walking steadily. Joedel did not see the white-haired landowner, for his eyes were fixed on his father's bleak face.

When he saw Mr. Eller, Clint said, "It's gone, Cap'n

Jim," waving his arm. "Our crop's done gone." His voice contained the knowledge of a deeper loss.

Joedel knew there were no plants anywhere to reset with; it was too late to replant anyway. He thought bitterly of the good stand they'd achieved by painful resetting, blistering their hands on the wooden pegs.

"Great Godfrey!" Mr. Eller exclaimed. "We're not licked, man. Not about to be." He reached in his pocket and, as if by magic, pulled out four new pocketknives. He handed each of them a shining knife, then flicked open the blade of his own, which flashed in the sun.

Walking to the end of the row, he glanced across the four acres of riddled plants. "Now," he said, "we'll cut the stalks back to the bottom leaf. When the sucker sprouts up, that'll be our tobacco stalk. We'll pour the fertilizer to it and raise it like a regular plant. It'll weigh out light, but it's better than no crop at all." Then he spit on his palm and bent to the task.

They had worked all afternoon cutting the stalks back, tossing them in the green-covered middles behind them. There was little talk among them, only when Sissie screamed at a hornyhead worm that had escaped the deadly hail. When his back was all one throbbing streak of pain, Joedel fell on his knees, crawling along from riddled stalk to stalk. It was the way Mr. Eller worked. The boy saw how Cap'n Jim's pants were ruined, his white shirt glued to his back with sweat. All of their thumbs were bloody from the numerous cuts.

Once his mother caught Joedel's eye, when they dropped behind Clint and Mr. Eller. She smiled and whispered, "Lord knows how he does it at his age, that man."

Three or four times, cars stopped by the road. The occupants stared at them working in the ruined field, shaking their heads. Then they started up and drove on.

By sundown they had finished the four-acre field, weary and crusted with mud. There was not a cloud in the sky.

When the boy held out the bone-handled knife, Mr. Eller said, "You handle that knife like a man, son. How'd you like to keep it?"

Joedel flushed and looked at his mud-coated bare feet. For weeks he had dreamed of a pocketknife like the one his friend Shag Squires boasted of, weighing the knife against the baseball mitt he hoped to buy.

"He thanks you kindly, Mr. Jim," Maddie said. "I reckon the cat's done got his tongue."

"Well, I got to go on and feed the stock." He paused long enough to tell Clint how to set the sweep when he next plowed the tobacco.

"I'll go help you, Cap'n Jim."

"Don't need any help," he replied shortly.

Clint stammered, "We're much obliged."

Mr. Eller walked across the field toward his car. Once he stopped and called back to them, "There's still a crop to be made here, if you're minded to work like Trojans. We can still talk about what we discussed yonder at the house."

Joedel watched his father's face break into a broad smile. "We ain't quit on you yet. We'll work it till the cows come home, Cap'n Jim."

Then they were all grinning, looking at the fresh field of tobacco stumps, the air scented with a green odor. Joedel ran his sore thumb across the knife in his overall pocket.

In the catalpa tree by the curing barn, a thrush began to sing, rinsing the evening air.

Joedel and Sissie buried the three biddies by the empty potato bank, using spools for tombstones.

After dark the Baptist preacher came. He had not called on them since their well had been poisoned, but now he appeared, since they had suffered from the Lord's own work. Neither Maddie nor Clint Shaw had ever attended his church, nor had they been asked.

They were sitting around the table, their bones aching from the afternoon's work. Joedel was cleaning the dried mud from his new knife, his sister's eyes wide at the shiny hawk's-bill blade.

They felt the front porch sag, then there came three knocks.

"Come in," Clint called.

In the yellow lamplight their heads turned to see the preacher looming in the doorway. The boy watched the tall rawboned man, his eyes lighting on the basket in his hands. He could not make it all out, but he saw that the basket contained food—a loaf of bread, potatoes, cornmeal, and more.

His mother spoke, but Clint Shaw lowered his truculent head, studying the cuts on his hand.

The dark-suited minister set the basket on the edge of the table. There was an embarrassed smile on his angular face and he mumbled something about hard times. Then with more confidence, "These are bad times for us all and will be till all God's children get right with the Lord."

"Amen," Maddie whispered.

The preacher said he had just heard of their calamity, God's visiting his vengeance upon their money crop. "You must recollect how the Lord moves in strange and mysterious ways. Be mindful of that. It's the pure Scripture."

"We're much obliged, Reverend," Maddie said softly.

Which is when Clint Shaw made his move, as Joedel knew he would. Without a word, he stood, swept up the basket of charity, then strode past the astonished preacher.

"You, Clint!" Maddie called, her dark forehead creased.

Joedel followed him as far as the porch. His father walked with his back stiff, without any hesitation, straight to the hogpen. As the boy watched—the others stood wordlessly on the porch—Clint Shaw dumped the food into the hog trough. They could hear the Duroc sow chomping into it, grunting with satisfaction.

Then he walked straight back to the porch, stiff-necked, his eyes not wavering.

The minister stood on the top step, his prim mouth gaped.

"Here's your goddam basket. Now git."

He took it. The black-suited preacher snatched it as Clint walked into the house, shutting the door. Joedel caught the look of scorn he turned on his mother.

The Baptist minister was walking, then trotting toward his car. He slammed the door, raced the motor, then the Model A wheeled crazily into the narrow road and was gone.

The children stood on the porch on either side of their mother, looking at the lightning bugs after the sound of the car had died away.

"Huh," Sissie said, "that's a preacher got gone. That's one old preacher got gone in this world."

"I reckon your pa did right."

But Joedel already knew that. He also knew that in the unlit bedroom behind them Clint Shaw was weeping soundlessly, his face cupped in his hurt hands.

"Joedel." His father was shaking his shoulder. "Wake up. It's auction day, son."

It was only a little past dawn when the boy awoke the second time. He had been dreaming of a lost hoard of gold coins, but when he reached triumphantly for them, suddenly they turned to crumbly vanilla wafers. The mournful quaver of an owl was mixed in with his deep sense of loss. When he opened one eye, there was not the platinum beauty of Jean Harlow casting its radiance on him from above his cot. Instead, there was only the advertisement tacked on the log wall, the moon-face of John Barefoot, owner of the New Deal Warehouse.

"Joedel." Clint Shaw shook him roughly. "It's time. It's time to stir, boy."

For an instant fear gripped him, and he thought he had fallen asleep and let the fire go out, spoiling the tobacco. But as he sat up on the gritty quilt, he heard the reassuring roar of the furnace and the crackle of hot flues. The temperature would be

19

over two hundred degrees now, the stems nearly all dried out.

Joedel stood up, rubbing the cobwebs out of his dark eyes. His shoulders were stiff and sore, for he had helped barn tobacco the day before for Mr. Eller, and he was not yet used to lifting the heavy crates from the mule-drawn sleds.

Just now Mr. Eller whistled shrilly from the Big House, and Joedel heard the Negro sharecroppers answer, as his father did, with a whistle or loud "Wahoo!" Across the flat fields and pastures he saw plumes of smoke coiling up from the scattered shanties. He imagined the little white-haired landowner standing near the magnolia tree at the two-story white house, whistling with two fingers stuck in his mouth. Cap'n Jim always went to bed with the chickens and was usually up at four o'clock, urging his tenants to the fields and barns.

Father and son waited under the open shelter as Mr. Eller sent a final importunate blast across the dew-drenched morning. Then Clint Shaw laced up his brogans.

"Listen at him. Ain't he something now, the Cap'n? Loud enough to wake up the devil." As usual, he spoke harshly, disguising his closeness to the old man whose farm he tended, the admiration and pride he would never articulate.

They grinned shyly at each other, fully awake now.

Joedel saw that Maddie's side of the bed was empty, only Sissie lay curled under the gritty sheet, close to the warm clay-daubed logs. His mother had already walked the two hundred yards to the tenant house to start their breakfast—and dinner, too, since they would be gone all day. He heard the rattle of the chain as she drew water from the well, and a pair of mourning doves in the pasture behind the Big House.

The boy turned to the door, then pulled the twine that his mother had braided from used tobacco string. When the thermometer bobbed against the dusty pane of glass, he peered at it, also noting how the middle flue was glowing a dull red from the heat.

"It's two hundred ten," he said, letting the warm twine slip smoothly through his fingers. He thought, If one of those sticks fell now across a flue—it would be the end of Papa's dream, forever.

"You climb up and check them stems. They ought to be pretty near dried out. They are, we'll let her cool down now, before we leave." His father blew the sooty lantern out, shaking it close to his ear to test how much oil remained.

Fully alive now to the possibilities of the day, Joedel climbed up on the dwindling stack of firewood, onto the tin shelter, then carefully up the ladder nailed to the side of the barn. When he reached the small wooden window under the gable, he paused for a moment. An ineluctable feeling of joy swept through him and he shouted a loud "Wahoo!" to the morning, his throat swelling like a rooster's. It was good to feel the old barn logs give under his weight. A chunk of clay came loose and thudded against the furnace below; a spurt of hot air shot out, tickling his patched knee.

He let his lungs fill with the dew-rinsed air, glancing across the wide, flat fields. There was enough light now to distinguish between tobacco, corn, and cotton, then, vaguely, the tall paper-shelled pecan trees at Mr. Eller's. He could see that the other tenants, all Negroes, were already scurrying about, preparing for opening day at the auction. He heard a trotting team and wagon on the clay road, headed for Clayton.

The boy's heart quickened, because for the first time he would have a basket of his own to sell at the auction, a gift from Cap'n Jim—even if it was damaged, slightly rotten. No, not really rotten, for he had picked out all the tainted leaves he could find. This day, he told himself, he would remember all the years of his life.

As the light of morning spread, he looked once again toward the tenant house, relishing the new perspective. He liked the old house, even though his mother did not, preferring the cotton-mill village they had left in Hoover times. Joedel felt as though he were looking down on the barns and sagging back porch from a great height, say, the red sawdust pile at Sam Eller's mill. The rail fence lot, smokehouse, and clay potato bank looked neat and clean; the hail-shredded sunflowers and sagging scarecrow in the garden seemed suddenly dwarfed.

He felt a surge of pride, for the weathered gray house was the biggest of all Mr. Jim Eller's tenant houses. The others were only three-room shanties with stunted outbuildings and small garden plots. Here was where the landowner had lived before the war, before he built the two-story "Big House" on the green rise, where soon the array of lightning rods would sparkle in the rising sun. Under the pecan trees a rooster crowed and, nearby, the boy's pet bantam answered.

"You, Joedel."

Quickly, he twisted the latch and opened the small board window, turning his face away from the blast of hot smothery air, his nostrils stinging with the scent of drying tobacco. His left arm broke into a sweat as he thrust it into the barn, his fingers fumbling above the top tier pole for leaves that were dry as locust husks. Each time he bent a stem end it broke with a snap, stiff as a dried twig. He broke three off to show his father, letting the window bang shut.

On the ground, Joedel wiped his face on his shirt sleeve, handing the three warm stems to his father. "They killed out. Those stems are dry as fodder."

"Yeah, they're dry as a old maid's kiss. We'll let her cool down now." Then he asked, "How does it look up there?"

"It's some kind of pretty, Papa. That tobacco's nothing but golden wrappers."

His father smiled and spat beyond the shelter. "Yeah. Cap'n Jim climbed up there yesterday, him at his age. Even he had to brag, though to be sure it's got no weight to it. Pretty as a guinea hen, but it's too light."

Joedel threw back the iron furnace door, and his father kicked open the two air holes on each side of the front door.

"Now we better get a move on. That market yonder ain't gonna wait on us." Already his father had heard the loaded wagons and trucks passing on the dirt road which led to the landing and ferry.

Clint Shaw picked his daughter up without waking her,

holding her close to his blue denim jumper. Joedel watched as his gaunt father strode through the wet weeds toward the tenant house.

"I'll be on directly to milk, Papa."

"Get the doors. I clean forgot the doors."

The boy opened both doors of the barn and propped them with tobacco sticks. Papa's as excited as I am, he thought, but he won't let it show.

For a moment Joedel squatted before the furnace, looking at the subsiding flames. Close to the furnace on live coals were the black coffeepot, and to one side the skillet with leftover squirrel and rice Maddie had cooked for their supper. He was not hungry, but the boy ate a spoonful of the peppery stew, savoring the tawny taste. Even cold, he liked it for the wild flavor of the squirrel his father had shot. Swallowing, it was as though he could taste the tangy heart of the deep forest.

He could kill squirrels, too, but still he could not gut them and dress them with the skill of Clint's cruel knife. It made him turn weak, just as he did when holding the shoats for his father to castrate, an ache in his groin. In this he was like Maddie, who could not wring the necks of chickens. His father always killed the fryers, laughing as they flew headless, flapping their wings against the garden fence, spilling blood on the worn earth like wet coins. Though he tried to hide his feelings, at such moments Joedel turned pale.

"You half-Indian," his father said harshly, "and you can't even wring a pullet's neck. I'll swear and be damned if it don't beat anything I ever heard tell of. You and your mama."

Joedel poured out half a cup of coffee and drank it black, making only a small face. He had learned to drink it without milk or sugar, like his mother and father, though now there was milk to spare.

Then he went to check on the rabbit box at the end of the garden, stepping through the wet pokeweed and burdock. The trapdoor had fallen, but there was no rabbit inside. He set it again, with the hum of early bees in his ears.

Then Joedel urinated beside the rabbit trap. In the open

he was always careful to urinate in a different place, for the salt would make the land infertile. It would kill the earth, his Indian grandmother had said, and to kill the earth was a terrible sin, like burning bread. Joedel reddened, for the hump-backed scarecrow in the garden seemed to turn its battered head toward him. Even the one-eyed martin gourds were facing his nakedness. He fumbled at his fly and hurried toward the house.

THE SUN WAS NOT YET UP. JOEDEL MILKED THE
brindled cow slowly, for he enjoyed milking. In the next stall he
could hear the two mules stomping, their teeth grinding the
few weevily ears of corn his father had given them as a tribute
to the special day. The cow slobbered as she switched her tail,
chewing on nubbins that were more cob than corn. Nearby, a
partridge called to its mate in the pine thicket.

The boy pressed his dark head into the cow's flank. Tilting the pail on his bare toes, he aimed the white stream toward
the corner. He liked to hear the jet of warm milk hit the pail,
then watch the quick foam as it rose steadily in the dented
bucket. Joedel's nose quivered with the pleasure of the milk
smell, as it did to green fennel or the cypress shingles he split to
build pyramidal bird traps. He did not mind when the cow's
tail, aimed at a buzzing horsefly, raked a cocklebur across his
copper cheek.

"Soo, there, Bessie, soo, gal."

He had carved the cow in a bar of Octagon soap for the
hobby and craft school fair last fall, idealizing her, for she had

only one hooked horn. The carving had not won a prize, but his arrow collection had.

He had not even thought to enter the collection of arrowheads until Doctor Clay's wife asked him to. She was the sixth-grade room mother and she had driven over from Clayton to ask him about his arrowheads. She was a tall handsome lady with frank blue eyes, her auburn hair drawn back in a bun.

Joedel liked her immediately. She had not made him feel like an Indian, a stranger in an alien land. She had merely suggested that he mount his collection and she was almost sure it would win a prize, saying she had learned of his hobby from DeWitt, her son.

And he had done it, with Mr. Sam Eller's help. He had mounted the arrowheads—flints, slates, all kinds—in an old Barlow knife showcase, with a spearpoint at the center. At Mr. Sam's suggestion they had glued them in so as to make the design of a huge arrow, poised in flight. It had won a blue ribbon, and for the first time he had been pleased to acknowledge the Indian blood that had brought his family nothing but trouble in Cape Fear County.

Joedel had blushed under the stares of his classmates as he stood up to receive the ribbon. The doctor's wife praised him for taking pride in his heritage. "After all, Joe Dell has a right to a special sense of pride. The Indians were here a long time before the white men came. And we all know that the Croatans are descendants of the Lost Colony—the first white settlement in America."

Joedel took the ribbon, thinking of the theater in Lumberton, where the Indians sat separately from both whites and Negroes.

Only a few clapped when he sat down, and Joedel noticed that the other judges were frowning at the homeroom mother, now presenting a ribbon to Trudy, a pretty classmate, for a slender vase modeled from red clay. He found himself staring at the red lips of Trudy's vase, and, blushing, looked at the back of the room-mother's head.

The doctor's wife had meant well, mentioning the widely known legend of the Lost Colony and tacitly accepting the theory that the boy's mother was descended from the mysterious Croatans. But, Joedel thought, she doesn't even know that we're no longer called Croatans. The name had come to mean only a mongrel race to be looked down on with contempt, in the end shortened to Cro by the neighboring Negroes and white farmers. Finally, the beleaguered remnants of the Croatans had given up their claim to being descendants of the English colonists and petitioned the Legislature to be called the Cherokees of Robeson County. (Later they would be renamed Lumbees.) Most people, like Mrs. Clay, were unaware of the new tribal name and the reasons for the change and went on calling them Croatans, the name the English found carved on the tree at Manteo when they discovered that the first colony had vanished into the wilderness.

His mother strained the milk through two layers of white cloth, pouring off the last into a half-gallon jar and screwing on the bright lid which she kept spotless. It was Mr. Jim Eller's jar of milk.

"You take that milk on to the Big House. And don't you waste time, Joedel." Breakfast would be ready when he returned and then they would load the tobacco on the Hoover cart. "You know how your papa is, always in a strut on auction day." She smoothed the feedsack apron over her bulging stomach. "And don't forget he said ask Mr. Jim about the tarpaulin."

"Yesum."

As Joedel walked the worn path along the ditch to the white house on the little hill, the sun began to rise over the tall longleaf pines. A few birds were already up, towhees and sparrows, scrabbling on the ditchbanks among the sumac and trumpet vines. The heavy dew was cool on his bare feet, the warm milk sloshing in the jar in the crook of his arm. The boy began whistling.

Every morning for more than two years he had taken the

jar of milk to Mr. Eller, not missing even once because of ill-
ness. He came to realize that the little Cap'n did not really need
all that much milk, now that his nervous and childish wife had
been taken to the State Hospital in Raleigh. No, Mr. Eller went
on buying the same amount because he knew they needed the
ten cents a day. Also, lately there was a growing family of cats
that slept under his back porch, and the old man kept a perma-
nent bowl of milk for them.

Joedel thought of the old lady whom he scarcely knew, a
skeleton of a woman with a hurt, severe face, a silvery bun at
the back of her head. He had seldom seen her in the house,
where she peeped out from behind curtains. Now it was said
she did not recognize Mr. Jim at all when he drove the ninety
miles to Raleigh to sit in the austere room with her. He had
overheard Clint and Maddie whispering this. Anyway, Cap'n
Jim drove up to Raleigh once a month, regular as clockwork,
though his daughters complained of his poor driving and said
his license should be revoked because of his age and weak eyes.
They were critical because he refused to give in and live with
one of them, preferring his freedom and the companionship of
Aunt Mary Mape, his Negro housekeeper.

The Big House sat back from the clay road, with scattered outbuildings and a huge tin-roofed barn on the opposite
side. The whole barn, roof and all, was painted white that was
turning a streaked gray. Joedel saw that the International truck
was already backed up to the barn, and Shadrach and the
Negro tenants were loading it, handing the tobacco down from
the second story, above the corncribs and mule and cow stalls.
He waved at Booster, Shadrach's son, who was his own age and
already a cropper making seventy-five cents a day in the fields.

Hurrying, he walked across the unkempt lawn, then
under the pecan trees and on back, where a Delco plant sat in
the garage, next to the dark-eaved smokehouse and two walnut
trees. Over the garage was the room where the old mulatto
housekeeper lived. Looking at the hammock made of barrel
staves and wire, Joedel remembered his dream of Blackbeard's

florins. Once he had found a handful of money under the crude hammock hung between the walnut trees. When he gave it to Mr. Jim he was rewarded with a shining quarter, which he had put in a Prince Albert can and hidden behind the cracked plaster by his cot. He had said nothing of it, for once when he'd found a dime in the road, his mother had bought a can of mackerel with it, saying, "Hoover times are hard times, son."

Her words seemed to echo in his ears as he knocked on the back door. For the times must be bad for Mr. Eller, too. His large square house was scaling paint and the screen on the wide back porch was rotting out, with unpatched holes open to the flies.

Mr. Eller had let things go after his wife was committed to the State Hospital. The chickens roosted in the walnut trees, their droppings falling on the hood of his old Studebaker. A brood of pigs had rooted up a crepe myrtle bush where the lightning rods were grounded on the south side. Inside, the floors were not always swept and the sagging furniture went half dusted, for the old colored woman had cataracts on both eyes and was a slovenly housekeeper.

The moment he knocked with his knuckles, calling "Mr. Jim," a half-dozen cats scurried from under the house, purring, and twining their tails around his patched overalls.

In the kitchen he heard Mr. Eller stirring around, eating his solitary breakfast. When he opened the door, Joedel caught the odor of bacon and coffee and the noise of the staticky radio.

Joedel saw that Mr. Eller had already put on his rumpled seersucker suit, white shirt, and black bow tie, his auction-day dress that never varied, as though it were a uniform. There were snuff stains on his right sleeve, and his black shoes were unpolished and turned over at the heels.

Until a light stroke and his daughters joined forces to stop him, the little Cap'n had toiled with his Negro share-croppers, sweating profusely, working harder than any of his hands in the hot, flat fields.

"I declare," his daughters would say, "Papa dearly loves

to go perfectly filthy." And they hinted that Mrs. Eller's nervous condition could be blamed on her husband, who never took time off from his work for vacationing or entertainment.

On the other hand, the Negroes took a fierce pride in the little Cap'n. "He don't ask us to do nothing he won't do hisself, that man." In the long cotton rows he would lead the field hands, his hoe setting a steady rhythm, sweat running off his prominent nose, staining his white dress shirt with salt. "Work? Do Jesus, look at that man go. Whooee!" And the Negroes would smile at each other, lift their hoes in the blazing sun and try to catch up with the white man leading them mercilessly under an old felt hat, pausing only to spit on his hands.

Now Mr. Eller opened the screen door and looked at the lanky boy on the back steps.

"I brought the milk, Mr. Jim."

"Come on in, son."

He took the half-gallon jar, slamming the door against the swarming cats and hitting Joedel's heel. For a moment he railed tenderly at the cats that threatened to inundate his home, asserting that the Lord had sent them as a curse on his head.

This was an early morning ritual and Joedel smiled. He watched as Mr. Eller poured out half the jar of milk into a cracked porcelain bowl and slipped it out the rusty screen to the hungry cats.

"There you are, sir. You greedy tom." Then to Joedel, "There's not a thing more pestiferous on God's green earth than a pack of mangy, ungrateful cats. They are a curse and a care."

"Yes, sir."

Joedel looked at the long table on the porch. It was piled high with vegetables brought by the tenants, now that Mr. Eller no longer tended a garden. Under the laden table were striped watermelons and warty orange squashes. At the end of the porch was a large blue vase with shedding sea oats in it and nailed to the wall a deer's antlers holding Mr. Eller's summer hats.

Aunt Mary Mape came out from the kitchen, an old woman with fierce hair and skin the color of a fig newton. She peered at Joedel through half-blind eyes, smiling.

"How're you, Aunt Mary Mape?"

"I'm fair to middling for a old woman, I reckon." She took the jar from Mr. Eller. Nodding at him, she said querulously, "You see he's going. He won't listen to Doctor Clay. He done told him he could miss one opening day in his life."

Joedel told her it wouldn't seem like an auction without Mr. Jim. Which was true; he hadn't missed an opening sale since before the war. And he had been the first farmer to plant tobacco in the whole township.

"You mind him to bring back my ointment from that yonder drugstore."

"Yessum."

Mr. Eller spoke. "You all got that curing ready to put on the floor?"

"It's ready, Mr. Jim. It's in good order."

Remembering Maddie's admonition, Joedel was turning away from the back door.

Mr. Jim asked, "What about your little basket? You gonna put it on the auction?" His voice was less severe, his thin lips smiling.

Joedel looked across the overgrown privet hedge toward the scuppernong arbor. "It's ready. I got it picked out and disguised good now. Papa says you all reserved space for my pile."

"I hope you have a good sale, Joedel, your first one," Aunt Mary Mape said. "I done said a prayer for you."

Joedel was embarrassed. He could not look the old man in the eye. If he did, he knew that he would give himself away, maybe his lip would tremble.

"I'm much obliged to you, Mr. Jim."

Mr. Eller did not even nod, for that was his manner, brusque. But before Joedel had rounded the corner he called after him. "Wait. You tell Clinton I'm sending Shad on with my two-horse wagon. I'm sending him on directly, and I mean for him to use it, hear?" Mr. Eller said he never intended to take any chances with that one-horse Hoover cart. The use of the wagon would cost the tenant nothing.

Then he added, "Tell him I can't spare any tarpaulin now."

"I'll tell him for you, Mr. Jim."

But he was frowning, for he knew Clint Shaw had his mind set on going to market in his own cart. He was that prideful—one reason he had refused to load up on the International truck—though the extra cost was the main consideration.

Clint had built the Hoover cart himself, using the rear axle and wheels of the Model A Ford they had moved to the farm with, selling the rest for junk during the first hard winter.

Joedel lengthened his stride. Still, the two-horse wagon would be faster; it would give them more time to spend in Clayton before the auction began. Maybe, on the way back home, Clint would let him sit up there and drive the team of white mules by himself.

Suddenly he began running toward home, clutching the dime in his pocket.

But he could not pass the curing barn without looking inside again. He bent in the open doorway, feeling the escaping heat across his ribs, filling his lungs with the sharp, pleasant odor. He peered in at the heavily veined leaves hanging on sticks from the poles, rising in tiers above the cooling flues to the roof. Now brittle as fodder, they had colored up yellow and orange, and he knew this cropping would bring the top price at the New Deal Warehouse, even if there was a depression on. Even a depression could not diminish the beauty of tier on tier of the golden leaves. More, he knew that he had had a part in the raising of the tobacco, and that it would make a payment on the piece of land his father had set his heart and mind on owning.

IV

"GREAT GODFREY, CLINTON," MR. JIM ELLER HAD said. "What do you want to buy a farm for? It's nothing but a botheration from one season to the next. It's nothing but a trial and a curse."

Clint Shaw wanted to broach the plan all winter, but the perfect moment had not presented itself. Three years earlier, plowing in the fields with Mr. Eller, he had looked at the bottom acres sloping almost imperceptibly to the shallow stream, but he could not bring himself to speak. Working in the fields together, there had grown between tenant and owner a subtle bond that comes to those who till the earth side by side. But no man speaks of such invisible ties, and Clint could not presume upon them, would not. Still, the dream took shape in his head, until it glowed like the preacher's bright lamp at church. Already he could see a three-room house on the little rise near the pine thicket, with the creek close enough to hear at night, after a rain.

Now he and Joedel sat in the crowded sitting room of the Big House, off from the musty parlor, the colored housekeeper sweeping and humming in a nearby bedroom. Clint had come to get the papers signed for the team of government mules. The old man was lonely and in a talkative mood. While the boy cracked stale pecans from the wooden bowl, he and his father had listened to Mr. Eller's tales of the years spent cutting the timber on York and Cat islands off the coast of South Carolina, before the war. That was where he'd found his "geechee" sharecroppers. Then when he told of returning to the farm, Clinton found the opportunity to mention his plan. He had blurted it out, knowing if he hesitated all would be lost again.

Joedel looked at the surprised face of the white-haired landowner, who sat short-legged and long-waisted in a wicker chair. His feet were in thick cotton socks, his black shoes beside his spitting box, which was wrapped in tinfoil. Behind him was the tall Victrola with the cabinet for the thick records that played when you wound the handle. Behind the Victrola was a long Civil War rifle, rusty with neglect, that had belonged to his father.

Joedel sat on the cluttered settee, and his father, in faded blue overalls, leaned toward Mr. Eller in a rocker, his felt hat beside him on the rugless floor. In the corner near the boy was a wicker table with a radio on it. On the shelf beneath were a big box of Railroad Snuff and a stack of old farm magazines, *National Geographics* and *Congressional Records,* for Mr. Eller had once been a county commissioner. The *Records* were unread but the Bible by the radio was well thumbed; he was still a deacon in the Presbyterian Church.

"That land ain't much account nohow, it's about played out." Mr. Eller had not shaved, and one hand felt of the bristles on his sharp chin, his pale blue eyes studying his tenant covertly.

Joedel looked at the liver spots on the old man's hand. They are like the spots on a puppy's belly, he thought.

Clint shook his head, as if to indicate that Mr. Eller had never abused an acre in his life, no more than he had a cow or mule or any animal.

"I don't know, sir. I want a place. It ain't for me—not just for me." He nodded toward his son. "I want that boy there to hold his head up. A man owns a little piece of dirt—I don't know, his childern grow up different." Then he added, "A piece of land lets a man be a man, no matter what color his skin."

Joedel felt the old man's periwinkle eyes on him. Embarrassed, he looked through the door at the big brass andirons at the far end of the seldom-used parlor. On the mantel was a pair of statues, a colonial boy and girl in blue, under a gilt-framed bearded patriarch. There were frilly curtains and dark stuffed chairs and an upright piano that Mr. Eller's youngest daughter had played.

The boy could not see beyond the glass doors, but he knew they opened into a large dining room where there were golden chimes between the tall windows, a gleaming table under the chandeliers and on the sideboard, beautiful blue and white china.

"Ain't I been fair to you these three years? You've not got any complaints?"

"No, sir. I can't say you've not treated us fair and square. It's just—I want something different for the childern, that youngun coming into this world before too——"

Mr. Eller interrupted to say he had been satisfied with Clinton's work, even pleased. He'd hired him from the cotton mill against his better judgment. "I'd a heap ruther have colored folks as sharecroppers, though you can't depend on them nowadays," he said, frowning. "But you turned out all right. Fact is, you're the best hand I got for curing. I've come to depend on you and Joedel there. You've not let the depression turn you to stealing or going slack, like some I could name." He said hard times had a way of bringing out the best in people, or the worst. You could judge a man by the way he stood up to adversity.

Joedel basked in this praise, as palpable as warmth, for he knew Cap'n Jim was niggardly with such words. He did not brag on himself or others.

"Work," the old man said, looking through the dusty window at the broad fields he had cleared by hand. "Nobody can speak enough for honest work. It never gets its due nowdays. If people would work, I guarantee you there wouldn't be all this labor trouble yonder in Detroit and so forth."

"Yes sir." Clint assured him that they would go on farming for him. They would just move out of the tenant house onto his own small place, maybe twenty acres, if Mr. Eller would spare that much on easy terms. "You can depend on us, Mr. Jim. We'll help you. That baby grows up, we're gonna have us a good force to put in them fields."

The boy watched his father rock back, relieved, his big hands straining together unconsciously as he said *force*. His fingers locked together across the bib of his patched overalls.

Mr. Eller smiled thinly. "You already got a good work force, Clinton. Any man would be proud of your force. Why, Maddie works in the field just like a regular—a regular Trojan."

Joedel stared at the landowner, who was caught in a moment of embarrassment. The boy thought, He almost said *nigger*. He almost said my mother works like a nigger, which is true. No, she works harder than any colored woman I ever saw. She is thirty-two years old and already looks forty, older than Papa. He looked at the deep lines cut from Clint's strong nose to his thin-lipped mouth, his sunken field-tanned cheeks. The hair on his forehead was thinning and dry and there was a bald spot on his crown. The hair just above his red ears was already turning gray.

"She works," Clint said. "It's hard times now. I hope it won't be like that for her always. Leastwise, not for the childern. A man has a kind of dream for his younguns. He don't want them to suffer—to go the path he has to walk."

Mr. Jim nodded, his blue eyes looking at the picture of his three daughters on the mantel, the photograph of his uniformed son who had died in the war. He leaned over and spat in the fly-ridden box, a trickle of snuff juice in his white bristles.

"It's the God's truth. I had it tough back yonder in the

old days. Sent my girls off to college, while my wife and me worked hard in the fields. Sometimes I think they don't much appreciate what all we done. At least, they seem to forget," he trailed off. He did not mention his son, who had planned to be a lawyer.

Clint scraped his brogans, for he saw they were getting away from the subject of the bottom acres that were now lying fallow.

Joedel looked at the wedding pictures of Mr. Eller's two older daughters, noting the paleness of their skins. He won't sell an acre, he thought, he'll keep it all for his own kin.

But his father took a breath and plunged ahead. "My folks owned that farm there across Slade Swamp. It made a difference when I was a little tyke. When you own your place, people look at you, they treat you—treat you different." He struggled but he could not find the words to express his meaning.

Mr. Eller nodded. "I knew your folks."

"They always voted for you when your name was on the ticket."

"That was a fine place they had."

"Seems like they never had any luck, once Pa took sick. Seems like everywhere we turned was a barbed wire fence."

The boy watched Mr Eller's bushy brows knit in a way that showed he didn't believe in luck. He was convinced a man made his own luck by sweat and toil. He said nothing, but all this was written clearly in his frown and thin crimped lips. When he frowned, the corners of his lips turned down and it was easy to see how much his daughters resembled him.

Joedel heard his father say that his mother had not lived to be a sharecropper. "When Pa died and the place went, she just naturally give up, like something in her curled up, secret, and died. We buried her in the family grave there, before the sheriff made us git."

Clint had joined the army soon after, which is where he acquired the tattoo on his right arm. After his discharge he had married Maddie, going by bus to Tennessee to avoid the state law against mixed marriages. Returning, he went to work as a weaver in the Badger Mill at Badgerville.

Then he told the old man of his other dream: to own a place of his own, then move the graves of his father and mother away from the lost farm, graves that were now covered over with broom sedge and blackberries.

Mr. Jim Eller didn't speak to that. He did not indicate whether he thought it was a foolish notion or not. "You so set on owning you a farm, why don't you see about maybe buying back your home place?"

Clint frowned. "I went to Clayton once to talk to old man McDougald. He wasn't interested in selling. He said maybe if I'd married my own kind—if the circumstances was different, he'd consider it. Said he owed it to the community not to sell the land to me or any of mine."

The little vein throbbed on Mr. Eller's forehead, and he pursed his lips. "I wouldn't pay any attention to that kind of talk. That old scoundrel is just land hungry. He was just casting about for any excuse. He don't want to buy up any land except that that joins his own property, and land's plenty cheap now. It's what's ruining us farmers, to say nothing of the land itself. Merchants that buy up the land and never live on it, never hold a plow handle in their hands, not even drive a tractor across it once. What do they know about the land, how to treat the earth right so it'll go on treating us right, us that have always lived on it and off it? They buy it and the land suffers, maybe dies. Folks move off it to town, and the land goes back to sedge and briars."

Mr. Eller got up from the wicker chair and walked to the littered mantel, not bothering with his shoes. He opened the heater door and spat angrily into it.

"You're mighty right, Mr. Jim. I'm one that don't aim to leave the land, now I've got back after all them years in that hell-fired mill."

Suddenly the white-haired man turned to face Clint, his back to the smoked photographs on the mantel. "How much land you reckon you gonna need?"

"I don't know, sir, Mr. Jim. That's up to you now. I figger maybe them twenty bottom acres yonder your croppers left when the barn burned. We'll take what's left on the crop and make a down payment. You know we've not got any money yet. But we got a good stand all around. It looks like a good year, and I'll have me them Roosevelt mules."

"It's gonna be hard, man. And it's gonna be up to you and your family." He said he was already committed to more than he cared to think about. He did not mention his wife in the State Hospital at Raleigh.

"I know that, Mr. Jim. But it's always been hard for us." Then he added, standing up, "It's not Hoover times any more. Poor folks like us, well, now they can start hoping again. It's about time, I reckon."

"All right, then. We'll talk about it when we straighten up at the end of the season." The two men shook hands on it.

"I appreciate it, sir." Clint Shaw could barely suppress a grin. He half winked at Joedel.

"It's my land, dad-burn it, and I ought to have a say. My girls won't need it all, they ain't going to live on it and soil their hands. It's my land, I say. I cleared those bottom acres with my own hands, with dynamite and one plug mule, before them consarned tractors were ever dreamed of. The Indians cleared it once and I cleared it after them, and I ought to have a say about what comes of it after I'm gone. Am I right?"

Clint was smiling for the first time. "You mighty right."

Joedel looked at his father standing tall under the high ceiling and the little Cap'n with his back to the three photographs of his pale daughters and uniformed son.

"We'll talk about it then and draw up some papers when the tobacco and cotton are sold. Mind you, I can't promise more than twenty acres."

"Yes sir, and we'll go on tending that farm for you, if you need us."

"I'm depending on you, man. I wouldn't make a deal

otherwise. I want to keep good people on the land. A cotton-mill town ain't no place to raise up younguns." He pursed his thin lips. "Lintheads."

At the front door, Mr. Eller frowned again. He put his hand on Clint's arm. "You know there might be trouble over this."

Clint replied evenly, "There's already been trouble."

Joedel saw his father's face grow stiff as cardboard. He knew he referred to the poisoned well and the note with three K's scrawled at the bottom. All because his mother was an Indian from Pembroke. All because her skin was the shade of a sponged tobacco leaf, and his and Sissie's. If it had not been for Mr. Eller's interceding, Joedel would have been forced to attend the Negro school at Winesap.

"I mean bad trouble if they find out you aim to buy land and settle in Ellers Bend."

"We'll have to cross that bridge when we get there then. For I mean to stay, one way or another, land or no land." Then he added quickly, "Lord willing and I do well."

Mr. Eller pressed his arm. "That's the spirit, man. Show 'em some spunk. I'll spread the word if there's any damn foolishness they'll have to answer to me for it. But it's you they'll be watching, not me. I don't know what makes them do such bastard things, but something drives them to it. Hard times as much as anything, I expect."

Clint said, "I'm not one to harbor hard feelings, Mr. Jim. All I ask is to be let alone."

Mr. Eller let his hand fall and changed the subject. He said he had always had sympathy for the Croatan Indians, since they were accepted neither by the whites nor other Indian tribes and seemed to mistrust most Negroes. "One thing I'll say for them, they've held on to their land up yonder at Pembroke."

Joedel followed his father down the front steps, between the small scaling columns, beneath the little banistered balcony. Beyond the boxwoods they paused in the shade of the pecan trees when Mr. Eller called from the porch.

"One more thing. Don't let it change you now. Sometimes a man gets a piece of land in his head and it warps him."

Clint smiled. "That can be the least of your worries, Cap'n Jim. I won't change none." Then he added, "Me and Joedel'll be up in the morning to plow that long cut."

But he had changed, Joedel thought. He had grown stingy, even cruel, now that he could hope that his dream would materialize. He had cut back on the groceries at Sam Eller's store. He refused to buy things for the house that Maddie needed, becoming angry over her request for curtains. They all wore clothes until they were too ragged to patch. He had even traded his guitar for an Oliver plow of his own. The boy noted that his father no longer whistled.

And he drove himself and his family as if a demon possessed him. That winter he and Joedel sawed wood and hauled it to Clayton in the Hoover cart, selling it for a dollar a cord. In his spare time his father found a job cutting crossties. When warm weather came Joedel and Sissie cut armloads of orange sedge, which their mother skillfully turned into brooms that sold for a dime each.

One day Maddie sighed, "He's a hard man, your father. Once he's got his mind set, he's stubborn as a pump handle. It seems like he don't think of the rest of us."

Joedel did not reply. He saw how cruel a dream could turn a man, yet he knew in his heart that sometimes an unbending stubbornness was right.

V

JOEDEL WAS NOT HUNGRY, FOR HE WAS FILLED with the promise of market day in Clayton. He sat anyway at the table in the cramped kitchen, which was always hot in August. Sissie sulked on the homemade bench beside him, sleepy-eyed, her pinched face darker than Joedel's, the deep copper shade of Maddie's.

His mother set the hot food before them and Clint Shaw began eating.

"Meat," he said. "By God, times may be rougher than a cob, but we always have something to putt on the table." He picked up the fried salt fish and tore at the meat with strong teeth, piling the delicately patterned bones on the worn oilcloth.

Joedel thought of how at school he has been taught not to say *putt*, the children around him snickering. Like the time they had discovered his mother's maiden name. "Oxendine, Oxendine, what sort of name is that?" they had chanted at recess until he had blazed furiously, "It's a Indian name and they were here before any white man ever dared come!"

In response, the children made a cruel ring around him, singing

"Oxendine, Oxendine
Wash their feet in turpentine."

Maddie went to the stove so she could replenish their plates. "Eat, son. It'll be a long day for you."

"I'm not much hungry."

"I reckon not. He's worrying about the little dab of tobacco yonder he's putting on the floor. Wondering if them buyers are going to smell the rot in it."

"It's not rotten, Papa," Joedel blurted.

"He's right, Clint, I helped him and——"

"No, but it was when Cap'n Jim give it to you, most of it anyhow."

The tobacco had been wet when a windstorm blew the tin back on Mr. Eller's big packhouse. It had gone unnoticed until one side of the curing was rotting under the sack sheets.

Joedel had slaved over the damaged leaves, even hanging them in the barn one Sunday and drying them out again, then sprinkling the hanks with Sweet Society snuff after his mother had tied them, helping him stack them evenly. Clint insisted that they keep the tainted pile far away from his good tobacco.

Would the buyers be able to detect the tainted leaves? He thought of the rows of sweaty men stooping and bending under the auctioneer's spiel, signaling on each side of the carefully arranged lemon and gold baskets. Thinking of the sharp-eyed speculators, the boy felt his spirits sink, his appetite gone. He wished the suspense was over. "I'll write *damaged* on the sales ticket," he told himself. "Then it will be settled once and for all." But he knew that he would not.

"His first sale," Maddie said quietly.

His baby sister frowned, spooning in the yellow grits and fish gravy.

Now his father was telling the story of Joedel's first trip to the Clayton market, how he'd dropped his hot dog when he stumped his toe crossing the Seaboard railroad tracks. "You remember how he come home and said, 'Ma, I stumped my toe and lost my dog.'" He had held onto the soggy bun, and that and a sack of boiled peanuts had been his lunch.

Clint threw back his dark head, laughing. "Stumped my toe and lost my dog."

Joedel had been teased with the story of the lost hot dog many times. Still he liked to hear his father tell it, basking in the warmth of his rough love.

Sissie made a face and said, "Silly," tossing her black hair.

"You hush up now, Sister. We'll get to go to that market before the season's over. Maybe they'll bring you a play-pretty from the Clayton store."

Joedel's scalp prickled as he thought of his first sale. He wished his mother and Sissie could be there. Perhaps there would be more than enough money to buy the baseball mitt, so he could buy a present for them, too. Once he owned the mitt, he would no longer be the last one called when they chose up sides at recess in the schoolyard, having to play whatever position no other boy wanted.

Presently he ate the salty fish and grits, the patties of lacy cornbread his mother had fried, chasing it with black coffee. The fish tasted good, once he shoved the thought of the shrewd pinhookers from his mind. Better, he thought, because he and Clint had caught them in the seine, salting them down in a lard stand. There were plenty more salted for the winter. But there were few fish left in the swamps and ponds, which more and more often were limed and dynamited, killing off everything at once, eels, minnows, and all. That was a sign of hard times, Clint said. Still, there was the trotline set in the mouth of Millers Creek.

Joedel avoided his father's inquiring eyes, putting off the subject of Mr. Eller's tarpaulin. Instead he looked at the squat

Dixie Belle stove, propped in front with two brick halves, ashes leaking through broken grates. Behind the stove on the smoke-darkened wall, his mother's shiny pots and black skillets hung on tenpenny nails. Over the wood box hung the milk bucket and damp straining rag.

When he'd finished eating, Clint picked his teeth noisily with a bone. Glancing at Joedel, he asked, "What'd Mr. Jim say about loaning us that tarp?"

The boy looked at his plate. "He said he hadn't any tarp to spare. Said there was plenty room in the truck for our barn of tobacco."

"I'll be John Brown." Clint gestured angrily. "I expected as much. Well, he can say on. I'll haul it my own way."

"Then he said be sure to wrap it good in quilts." He decided it was not an opportune moment to bring up the two-horse wagon.

"He's not got to send word for that."

His mother did not like the idea of sending all her good quilts to market. Frowning, she said, "I don't know why you don't just load it on Mr. Jim's truck. It would save a heap of——"

"Save nothing." His father's blunt jaw was set stubbornly. "I ain't paying to have my tobacco hauled, not when I got a perfectly good cart out there and them Roosevelt mules."

"Clint, it's only a penny a pound. It's——"

His father stood up. He said evenly, "He'll get his penny a pound all right, more than that. But it'll be a payment on my—on our land, Mama."

Maddie bristled and the boy saw her eyes flash. They were as gray as oysters in her high-cheeked coppery face. "You got land on the brain seems like, and there's no reasoning with you. If it was me, I'd settle for a new tablecloth and some curtains to hang in that parlor window, or a radio to listen at. I wouldn't set my notions so high, not with times being so hard, people going hungry all around us."

Joedel thought of the Negro tenants who had killed a mule and eaten it before the landlord found it out. He had heard the talk at Sam Eller's store. There were other sharecroppers who lived in packhouses, even old dirt-floored tobacco barns.

"These ain't Hoover times no more, Maddie. Things are looking up now. There's a *man* for a change up there in Washington, a Democrat. We got cause for hope now."

"Times might be looking up for some folks. They're not for us poor sharecroppers."

"That's just it," Clint said, quietly but fiercely. "We're not going to be croppers all the days of our lives."

"We'll see." His mother shoved at a strand of black hair with the back of her hand, her forehead creased.

"We got us a team, ain't we? We got Mr. Eller's promise on the land. And we gonna have a sale this day that'll putt Shad and the rest of them croppers' noses out of joint. You'll see, I tell you."

"Well, we'll see." Her anger subsided, the lines beside her straight nose softening. "I've got you some dinner fixed, such as it is. There in the stove warmer."

While Clint was angry, Joedel could not mention Mr. Jim and the wagon. He watched as his father stomped out the back door to hitch the mule to the cart.

Maddie turned to Joedel. "You now," she said. "You're not going to town looking like that. Put on some shoes and brush your hair back. " She had laid his clean blue jeans out on the cot while he milked.

His mother called after him. "Spruce up, boy, and hold your head high. Make them people in Clayton think you're as good as anybody. We might be sharecroppers, but we've not got to act like poor tacks."

Joedel started to protest, but he relented. "All right, Mama."

Before he could turn away, his mother told him to hold

still. Using her sewing scissors she snipped away the hairs that
stuck out above his ears, running her strong fingers roughly
over his head.

In his room he quickly put on the clean dungarees and
blue chambray work shirt, taking off the shirt and worn overalls he'd slept in at the barn. Sitting on his cot, he put on
fresh socks and tennis shoes. Then he combed his hair in the
mirror he'd hung on the nail over the shelf where he kept his
arrows and fragments of pottery. The mirror was cracked, cutting his image in half. He roached his coarse hair straight back.
His sideburns came down like his father's and under his black
hair, which stuck up on the crown, his skin was blue-black.

The boy's cot had been shoved against the peeling wall
to make room for the piles of tobacco, for his father would not
trust it in the old packhouse, once it was graded and tied and
ready to be sold. Maddie had protested, but he was too afraid it
would get wet or someone would break in the packhouse and
steal it. He wanted the tobacco in a safe place, where the hound
could guard it at night while they were curing the next cropping. Joedel looked at the waist-high pile, wrapped in ragged
quilts. His pulse quickened when he saw his own sheeted pile
in the far corner.

The boy looked at the picture of Jean Harlow, and her
smile seemed inexpressibly radiant, as if she were wishing him
luck at the auction. All of the walls in his room were plastered
with newspapers and pages from farm magazines. At first his
mother had despised it, saying "Niggers" the day they moved in,
for a Negro family had preceded them as sharecroppers, her
nose quivering with the funky odor. She had ripped the paper
away from all the rooms except Joedel's, where the cracks in
the wall were large and numerous. With the cold winds of winter, Maddie had relented, and she and her son put up new layers
of paper, making a lumpy paste of water and flour. It had been
a blow to her pride, and she was glad no company came to welcome them to Ellers Bend. She did not associate with the Negro
women, and the white women did not call on her.

But her son had come to like the papered wall of his little room. It was pleasant to open his eyes in the morning under the radiance of the movie goddess and he enjoyed reading the advertisements for Postum, Coleman Lanterns and Calumet Baking Powder. It was like looking at Maddie's catalogue all at once, and he soon memorized the prices of the new cultivators and the Farmall 30 tractors.

His mother kept only the parlor clear of newspaper, pasting a color picture of Whistler's Mother above the mantel. This she saved from the cover of *The Progressive Farmer* because Clinton had told her that the painter's mother had lived near Clayton, in a house that was now torn down except for the main chimney. Joedel knew the place well because once the fourth grade had gone there on a picnic and the teacher had made a little talk about Mrs. McNeill and how she ran the Yankee blockade at Wilmington to join her famous son in Europe.

As the boy finished plastering his hair down, the Negro backed Mr. Eller's two-horse wagon up to Joedel's bedroom window, reining the sleepy mules skillfully, avoiding Maddie's red canna lilies. It was bright day now, and Joedel watched the dark mustached Negro as he took the mules out of harness, jerking the hamestrings loose with one sure motion. Like his father, the colored sharecropper wore patched blue overalls and rough brogans.

"Shad, bruise one of them flowers and there'll be hell to pay with the old lady," Clint said. "I wouldn't give a plug nickel for your life."

"No suh!" Shadrach laughed easily. "I ain't so much as touched them pretty flowers." He was a wiry, bandy-legged South Carolina Negro and spoke with a "geechee" accent.

The boy buckled his belt and hurried outside.

"I didn't ask Cap'n Jim for the loan of that sorry wagon." The angry lines were etched sharply beside the white man's nose.

"I know that, Mistuh Clint. It just he don't trust that old cart of yours. The Cap'n says not to take any chances with that old Hoover cart this day—not with them yellow wrappers of yours."

"Hunh. That cart'll be there till Gabriel blows his horn."

Joedel was glad of the change in plans, in spite of his father's hurt feelings. Maybe he could drive the team all the way back, once the precious cargo was unloaded and sold at the auction.

Now he recalled the day he and his father had walked the five miles to Clayton. He had helped him pick the two mules out of the milling mass, stiff-eared and scared, in J. T. Cox's corral, watching while Clint proudly signed the papers. Many of the other sallow-faced farmers could do no more than make an X.

"Them's a fine pair you got there," the fat man with the plaited leather whip drawled. He had a burnt matchstick in his mouth and spoke without removing it. "They won't let a nigger have a white mule like that. In Georgia where I come from, if a darky owns a white mule, they make him say, 'Git up, *Mistuh* Mule.' It's a solid fact."

Then the fat man glanced uneasily at Joedel's frozen face, holding back his laugh.

They had ridden the government mules home bareback, in almost total silence, taking them across the silver bridge and the long way home to avoid frightening them on the little ferry at Ellers Bend.

Now, in the yard, Joedel could see his father's square-jawed face, the vertical lines in his forehead showing his irritation at the landlord.

"You come on, Mistuh Clint, and let's load your baccer on that big truck. They's plenty room left. Mistuh Jim said as much."

Clint scoffed at the notion. "We done went through that once. I ain't paying out a dollar a hundred hauling charges. When I got me two young mules in the stable yonder."

"The Cap'n say you that stubborn. He acted right put out. Me, I ain't studying no penny a pound totin' charges."

"No, you're gonna ride to market in grand style, while me and Joedel ride in this here old wagon."

Joedel knew it would hurt his father's pride to drive a borrowed wagon up the warehouse ramp when many of the white farmers drove trucks or trailers.

"What else did he say?"

"He acted right riled, Cap'n Jim did. Said he'd ruther have a nigger farming for him any day than a white sharecropper."

Joedel smiled at the way Shadrach said "nigger."

"You mighty right he had," Clint flared out. "Because he can make a nigger jump when he says jump, and me—I got a mind of my own. I got the gumption and grit to cross him when I strike a notion."

"Don't put that washing out now, t'ain't clean. Cap'n Jim don't make me jump none. It just I want to get my baccer on that floor yonder. I don't want to take any chances dawdling along the way, maybe get caught in the rain and that old tarp so leaky."

"How come, I want to know?"

Then Joedel saw that his father's tone had changed, that he was teasing Shadrach Gillings, his eyes crinkling. Besides, he was not really angry with Mr. Jim Eller, though at times he did flare up.

"How come you in such a all-fired hurry to get that trashy leaf on the floor? I'll bet the buyers won't even stoop to bid on it. Why, it won't even makes good snuff, not even poison for mites."

Shadrach looked at Joedel in mock disbelief. "What you spreading now, Mistuh Clint? Whose baccer's sorry? Man, you know my lugs cured out yellow as honey. You hear the Cap'n bragging on them golden wrappers yourself. I ain't hearing you spread such trash about my good baccer."

Clint winked at Joedel. "It's so black and ugly he took it out of the barn before day so nobody could see it, him and his younguns, and sneaked it in the back road. I declare half of the barn went in the pig lot."

"I swear to God." The Negro sharecropper was laughing now, holding the reins loosely under the chinaberry tree. "Listen to your papa, Joedel, if you want to hear trash."

"I just hope and pray the Cap'n ain't got my space reserved on the same row with all your piles of trash. The buyers might strike a notion my golden weed belongs with your sorry tobacco. That's how come I ain't hauling with you all on that truck."

"Listen at that white man, will you?" Shad's shoulders were heaving, his white teeth flashing. Already he was turning the brown mules in the yard.

Shadrach was leading the mules toward the road when he stopped. Joedel thought he might mention the pile of tainted tobacco he was taking to the auction for his first sale.

"I told him I'd as lief drive the mules, Mistuh Clint. But he say no, he won't trust me with his good wagon. That's how come I'm using the truck like them others."

"Go ahead on, man, before he starts that infernal whistling again. I can't stand here all day listening to your excuses."

Then he called after the grinning Negro. "You all be sure and hold my space on the floor for me, hear now?"

"We'll do that thing, sure, Mistuh Clint."

The opportunity had passed. Shadrach had not thought to mention Joedel's first sale.

VI

THEY BEGAN PASSING THE UNWRAPPED SHARP-smelling tobacco to Clint in the two-horse wagon. Sunlight caught the pressed leaves as Joedel handed them through the propped window, and the long-veined leaves were like beaten gold, like the gold figure in a photograph he had seen of King Tut's tomb in Egypt.

"By damn, handle that stuff with care, I tell you, boy."

"I'm not bruising it, Papa."

"It ain't nothing to play with now. You all just take care and keep it coming through that window. I already heard Rance Squires pass by a while ago in his ramshackly wagon. I tell you that auction ain't gonna wait on us."

For a moment they were serious and quiet—and with reason. For it is their life's blood, these thin leaves of tobacco which the family lifts, holds, and passes now, careful as if they were handling precious thin-shelled eggs.

As the sun edged over the tall pines beyond the field of tasseled corn, light fell in the clean-swept yard, on the weather-beaten frame house, its shingled roof, green-spotted with lichen. The four of them were silent a moment, hushed as the radiance caught the orange-yellow tobacco. It was gold answering to gold, the thin tapering leaves beautiful in the morning light.

The boy held a stick of tobacco out to the new sun to catch the falling light. He felt his arms ache with the weight of it, and remembering his dream of the pirate's coins, he wondered how much money it would bring at the auction. Maybe fourteen or even sixteen cents a pound. It had gone higher than that, the best grades, before Hoover times set in.

He passed the loaded stick on to his father in the wagon, watching him, too, hold it to catch the full light. Joedel glimpsed here and there a speck of ocher or brown islands in the gold the size of small butter beans. But the "frog eyes" did not matter really; they only intensified the yellow in the leaf's thin body.

Clint Shaw held the sharp-scented tobacco for a moment against the sun, close to his faded overalls, one strong hand at each end of the three-foot stick, tilting his dark head. Joedel did not need to see him to know the flecks of pride in his eyes. He smiled at his mother.

The bantam rooster crowed in the backyard, near the smokehouse, and Clint leaned forward and dropped the pressed tobacco in place on the growing pile. As the stick fell expertly in place, overlapping the last one, his breath was forced out, "hanh." He flattened his wide hands, stood on tiptoe, and let his weight press down.

"Pass that tobacco on," he said gruffly. "Don't play with it, boy."

It was Clint who had broken the rhythm of work and Maddie smiled back at Joedel, brushing the fine dust from her apron, stirring fresh motes in the sunlight. Then they returned to the old unfaltering rhythm. Almost silently they moved with the ritual motions: mother to son to father on the wagon bed.

As his mother stooped to the diminishing pile, the pressed leaves came apart with the sound of tearing silk, followed by the noise of her bare feet on the sandy bedroom floor as she turned to thrust the stick toward him. As she let go with her left hand, the stick began to fall, but the boy's hand was already under it. Joedel pushed the laden stick through the window, breathing the strong scent that would cling to the curtains in his bedroom until winter.

But he did not mind, for it was a good clean smell. It is the scent of money, he thought. Beyond even that, it is the odor of bread and meat on the table, of school tablets and new denims, of petticoats and ribbons for Sissie. And more important, a first payment on the land for his father.

"Papa, I'm picking up these leaves for you." Sissie walked around on the gritty floor picking up the short scattered leaves that had fallen from loose hanks, bunching them in her small fist.

"That's right. All us got to help get ready for that market yonder."

"Sissie's a sleepyhead." Joedel looked at his sister's black eyes. "Her eyes are still glued together."

"I'm not a sleepyhead. I stay up at that barn to help Papa cure this old baccer." She held up the bright leaves.

Maddie smiled. "One thing sure. She nearly pushed me off of that bed when that screech owl hollered. Sister shoved me clean against the wall, to where the heat wouldn't let me more than doze."

"Fraidycat," Joedel teased. "Sissie's nothing but a fraidycat."

"Hush now," Clint said.

"They say when you hear a owl like that, it's a sign someone's going to die," his mother said. There was a moment's hush, with only the whisper of the supple leaves passed between them. "I remember when my mama got down sick . . ." Her voice trailed off.

"It's Joedel's old coon. I hope it——"

"Thats enough of that," Clint said. "We've not got time for any such notions." It was clear that he did not approve of his wife's superstitions.

"I'm not afraid of any old owl."

Frowning, Clint Shaw said, "I said that was enough, now. You all pass them sticks on."

"Don't you say nothing, Joedel. You woke me up twice talking in your sleep. 'Head him off,' you hollered. 'Head off that mule.' As plain as that."

"Huhh," Clint said. "He's worried about that mule breaking loose and turning over a crate up there in Cap'n Jim's field."

It was true. The spilled-over crate of tobacco was a blow to his pride. He would never forget the gibes of the croppers as they helped him gather up the broken and scattered leaves.

His sister sulked and quit picking up leaves. "I'm going to market with Papa and Joedel. I'm going to set on that best grade at the auction."

Maddie said firmly that she could not go. "We'll go later on, Sister. They'll be so crowded on opening day you and me'd get stomped on. Our day'll come later. Besides, I need you to take off tobacco for me to grade today."

"I ain't studying taking off any old baccer. I'm going to ride to that market. Set up yonder beside Papa." Her lips were trembling.

"You going to get your backside warmed up if you don't hush," Joedel said.

"Your mama needs you to help her start on that next curing. You be smart, we gonna bring you a play-pretty from Clayton."

Sissie flounced her hair and walked over and kicked Joedel's little heap of tobacco.

"Mama, you see her bruising my tobacco. I'm gonna bruise her little butt directly."

"Hush that racket, I say."

"Huh," Sissie said. "Already bruised. Joedel's old baccer is plain-out rotten." She held her nose as if smelling a rotten egg.

"It is not so rotten."

"Mr. Jim didn't give you nothing but old rotten lugs

from the bottom of his pile. He ain't giving you no good baccer. Ain't it so, Mama?"

"That may be so," Joedel countered. "But I got them doctored up good now. That tobacco's gonna bring me a good piece of money."

"It ain't nothing but a stinking mess." Tears were brimming over in her dark eyes.

"Child, child, you hush now. You, too, Joedel."

Clint Shaw said, "It may be doctored all right. But I mean for you to keep your pile separate now, every leaf and stem of it. I don't want it near any of my good primings, not even to touch them. Them sharp buyers get one whiff of that on mine, then they'll use it as an excuse to steal our whole cropping. By damn, then school will be out for sure."

"Yes, lord. Some sorry pinhooker'll get it for next to nothing. All our work for nothing."

"No they won't. We'll turn the tag," Joedel said. "We'll bring it home this evening."

His mother flared up. "And what'll we do with it then? We can't wear it, we sure can't eat it."

Clint interposed, "Mama, we'll cross that bridge when we get there."

Joedel thought of the rightness of what his mother had spoken in anger. Tobacco was not like any other crop under the sun. It wasn't like cotton or corn or sugar cane. All that care and labor, and in the end it went up in smoke. Exhaled from somebody's lungs, or else spat out in nasty snuff spit by old women. Sometimes he would pause in the field and wonder if maybe Jean Harlow would smoke a cigarette made from one of their stalks. Somewhere was the girl he was going to grow up to marry; maybe in a few years she would inhale into her body some of the very leaf he had plowed and cured.

Finally, they were extra careful with Joedel's tainted gift from the landowner. Clint wrapped his tobacco in Maddie's handmade string quilts, then put an extra counterpane on top. Joedel's tobacco was passed through the window last, longer leafed than his father's, eight sticks of it, then wrapped in tow-sack sheets, with burlap bags tossed across the whole load, then a final Star of Bethlehem quilt.

The boy saw his mother's lined forehead as she studied the quilts that wrapped the load of tobacco. She was frowning, and he knew that she did not like to send her quilts to the Clayton market. They had been in the family longer than he could remember, and he recalled seeing the quilting frames hanging from the ceiling in his grandmother's house in Pembroke. Once he had helped his Grandmother Oxendine beat the cotton lining with little sticks. But his father set no value on the legacy of womenfolk. He could not afford a tarpaulin, so the quilts would have to serve and take their chance of being stolen during the bustle and scurry of the auction.

As they finished the loading, a pair of quail was calling in the pasture by the deep woods.

VII

Joedel watched his father step on a wheel spoke, then the protesting wagon tongue. With slow deliberation he sat down and took up the plow lines. Under the faded blue jumper his back was straight and under his straw hat his dark hair glistened with the water he'd dipped his comb into. Clean-shaven, he was wearing his newest overalls, and Joedel noticed that he'd greased his worn brogans with a piece of tallow.

The boy sprang up on the bale of peanut hay. He was grinning, trying to contain the excitement, feeling his heart beat faster.

"You feed old Coonie for me, Sissie?"

On the porch, his sister stood by her mother, her black eyes shimmering. Hands on hips, she stuck her tongue out.

"You ready back there?" Clint called.

"Wait!" his mother cried. "Lord have mercy, you've forgot your dinner."

Joedel took the brown paper bag and made a place for it under the quilt on the bale.

"You all mind my good quilts, now."

"Look for us when you see us, Mama," Clint said. "You know how that Clayton auction is."

Then they were off, at last. Clint Shaw lashed the team with the plow lines, and Joedel felt the wagon lurch, the axle grating. They were on their way to the Clayton market, his first sale, and he could not suppress the tingling in his shoulders. Wishing his mother could witness his moment of triumph, he glanced away from the figures on the slanted porch, letting his legs dangle, swinging them nervously.

Instead of his mother, Joedel looked at the clean field of cotton. Before long now frost would come, hardening the bolls and withering the green leaves. Then suddenly the field would turn beautifully white, a white cloud lying flat and still as far as Mr. Eller's old garden plot, where the stalks shot up too tall and rank, higher than his shoulders, as though reaching for the low branches of the pecan trees.

He liked to pick the cotton. Already he looked forward to October when his father would make new picking bags, tying the straps to newly washed guano sacks, which his mother had hung out on the garden fence to dry. He liked to feel the soft pliant lint yield to his eager fingers, to feel the tug of the filling bag on his shoulders. When his back grew tired he would kneel over the dripping white bolls, his ragged knees against the warm earth. He would work feverishly, trying to keep pace with his father and the skillful Negro hands.

Picking cotton and stacking peanuts were the only two times Clint Shaw kept him home from school—and then against his mother's wish. At first he did not mind; he felt important staying home to do a man's job. Yet when the orange school bus passed the field and the children yelled, jeering at him, he flushed, lowering his head to the open sack. Joedel was filled with a vague inexplicable sense of shame. Thereafter, until the cotton was harvested, at school bus time he ducked between the rows of dry stalks, like a fox peering slyly through the frostbitten leaves at the schoolchildren who searched for him among the Negro cotton pickers.

Before they reached the clay road, Joedel discovered the hound following them, sneaking up a corn row where field peas had been broadcast in the middles.

"Get on back!" he shouted. "If a oil truck hit you, you'd be nothing but a greasy spot on the road."

"Chunk him," Clint ordered.

Jumping off the wagon, he landed on the balls of his feet, little needles shooting up his legs. The spotted hound stopped, one foot poised in the air, brown eyes alert.

The boy began throwing at the puzzled dog. First he threw a peach pit, then a flattened snuffbox and the rusty tooth of a harrow. The iron tooth raised a spurt of dust before the baffled hound, causing a yellow and black butterfly to veer crazily.

Joedel smiled as the dog turned, trotting toward the house with its tail tucked between its legs. When the hound cleared the field, he looked back at Joedel, who slapped his knee loudly. Then the dog wheeled, chasing the yellow tom across the bare-swept yard and up the chinaberry tree.

Joedel had to run to overtake the slow-moving wagon. Bounding up beside the hay bale, he waved at the diminishing figures of his mother and baby sister. Then he pretended the quilts needed his attention, smoothing out the six-pointed Star of Bethlehem, his mother's favorite.

At the side of the narrow road, Joedel looked at the little open shed he and Clint had built for him to wait under for the school bus in raw weather. It was made of slabs and dark warped tin from a burned tobacco barn, no larger than an outhouse under the longleaf pine. The little shed was associated with painful memories. The school bus had not even stopped for him the first day. It had only slowed down enough for the pimply driver to shout, "Catch the jigaboo bus, dark boy." Joedel had waited patiently in the shed three days as the orange bus roared by, the children shouting and laughing at him. It stopped only after Mr. Jim Eller drove his old Studebaker to Queen City, the county seat.

One night a week later the little shed had been dynamited. He and his father had built it back, working silently under the tall pine. It had not been dynamited again and the school bus never failed to stop, though the driver remained sullen.

As soon as they crossed the culvert and the wagon grated onto the narrow clay road, Joedel took off his tennis shoes and tight denim coat. He wrapped the shoes inside his blue jumper, placing them beside the grease-splotched bag.

The mules picked up their stride and he saw that the journey would be a smooth one, almost as smooth as if they were riding to market in his father's Hoover cart with its inflated Model-A tires. The road-drag men had worked the road the day before, scraping it and filling in the worn ruts.

Joedel liked to see the yellow road machine clearing the ditches and turning up fresh-smelling clay like a huge insect monster. The two men who worked the machine never failed to let him ride if he was walking to Sam Eller's store, for they were as friendly as the one-armed Watkins salesman who always stopped to give him a ride, his old flivver redolent of vanilla extract and spices. He liked to stand behind the tractor and watch the curved blade, as long as the middle flue at the curing barn, turning the clay effortlessly.

For a while the boy let his legs dangle, his eyes taking in how the red clay sometimes turned to streaks of gray then back to orange-red, noting the powdery cloud stirred by the wagon wheels, the thin layer of dust on the early goldenrod by the ditch, the occasional flattened toads. Then he fished a peanut from the hay and ate it.

His father took off his jumper and tossed it over the tobacco. Already there were sweat stains between his shoulder blades.

Joedel saw him glance once at the bottom acres he hoped to buy from Mr. Jim Eller, then jerk his eyes away, keeping them straight on the road. Clint Shaw did not like to look at the land now lying fallow, the small flat fields growing up in broom sedge and blackberries.

Joedel did not mind looking; there was not much to see. A little pasture with a persimmon tree near a hog wallow, three or four fields with the ditch banks growing up in sumac and sassafras, a pine thicket beyond the little creek. The tobacco barn had burned last season and no one had cleared the twisted tin away from the caved-in furnace. The tenant shack stood alone between two whitewashed chinaberry trees, doors open and windows broken out. It still smelled of the Negro tenants who had quit farming to go north, and he knew his mother would never consent to live in it. But that was not his father's plan anyway. He planned to build a new house on the little rise and convert the clapboard shanty to a packhouse for their cured tobacco.

Late at night Joedel had heard Clint telling Maddie how much cotton he'd make to the acre, how many pounds of tobacco. He had not heard her reply, for she kept silent, waiting for the Badger Mill to reopen so she could prevail on him to return and live in the town west of Clayton, closer to her Indian kin.

Joedel settled his back against the layers of quilts, finding a place where no stick gouged him. The morning air was clean, washed with a heavy dew. Now the birds were out in full force, and he heard a towhee scratching up leaves in the undergrowth. The morning-glories were open, climbing the fences, higher than the orangy goldenrod.

As he looked at the few scattered farms this side of the swamps, everything looked new, somehow different. He had lived in Ellers Bend only three years, but already he knew every household, black and white. Even the fields had names for him, for Clint Shaw had at one time or another exchanged labor with each of his neighbors in order to get his own crops harvested. The swampy woods he and his father had hunted for squirrels and opossums and coons, and the network of creeks they had fished, or, with Shadrach Gillings, seined at night, salting the surplus perch and pike against the hard winter when money would be scarce or nonexistent.

The first farm they passed, beyond the fields owned by Mr. Jim Eller, was the Creed Duncan place. It was abandoned now, the two-story frame house sagging under four giant oaks, the flat fields going back to yellow sage, fennel and pine seedlings. From the creaking wagon Joedel could see only the swaybacked shingle roof.

But he did not need to see. He knew how things had gone to wrack and ruin the year old man Duncan died with cancer. All of his children left and soon the Negro tenants scattered. It was rumored that before they left they killed the remaining mule and ate it. One Sunday Joedel and his friend Shag Squires had sneaked behind the house to eat the scuppernong grapes in the fallen arbor. When they pried open a window they found in the attic only a clay Indian pipe, a few flint arrows, and some letters with postmarks that went back to Civil War days. They had soon left, for the house was reputed to be haunted. The story was told that when the mourners came home from Mr. Duncan's funeral there was a white dove in the room where he died. His son, an engineer come home from Texas, opened the window and the family stood in the silent yard watching as the white dove disappeared in the sky. It was a story retold and savored at Sam Eller's store.

The wagon lumbered past the Pentecostal Holiness Church, a small white building that sat in a stand of tall pines. Joedel looked at the scaling, truncated steeple, then the scattering of tombstones, white seashells outlining some of the graves, half-hidden by the sparse sedge.

The last farm before the swamp was owned by Kirk Wiles, who only pretended to make a crop, covering up for the illicit still he had hidden back in the swamp. He tended a half-acre of tobacco and a few acres of corn and soybeans, not even half-plowing them, often letting his crops go to Johnson grass and cockleburs.

The first winter Clint farmed for Mr. Eller, Kirk Wiles had driven his ramshackly wagon over to borrow their scalding barrel. The next week, hunting squirrels, Joedel and Clint had discovered Kirk's new still by a narrow creek. No one was tending it, so they walked up to the cold boiler. There was their scalding barrel filled with souring mash. Without a word, Clint turned the barrel over, threw it across his shoulder, and walked home with it.

Two nights later, someone poured kerosene in their well. The next morning on the porch they found a crude letter that said white men that married Croatan women were not welcome in Ellers Bend. There were three K's down at the bottom of the note, but Mr. Jim Eller said nobody needed to guess twice at who did such a sneaky stunt. Still, that had been only the first of his father's troubles. Before long, Maddie grew sullen, wishing to move away. At Sam Eller's store Joedel noted that the men barely spoke to his father, who withdrew into himself, making no effort to be friendly. He no longer traded work with anyone except Cap'n Jim's Negro sharecroppers.

Two hundred yards beyond the moonshiner's house, Joedel saw the snake track slithering across the road. "Water moccasin," he said aloud, a cold shiver at his spine, though it might have been only a harmless water snake. All along were bird tracks in the powdery dust, like a delicate stitching.

Soon he saw the cumbersome tracks of a small turtle—and there he was huddled in his carapace. Quickly Joedel slid off the wagon, scooped up the terrapin, then caught up with the plodding team.

The terrapin struggled to escape, wiggling his leathery legs and thrusting out his horny beak. The boy laughed out loud, holding him firmly, studying the yellow and brown design on its hard shell. When he turned it over he saw the beautiful yellow-and-black smoothness of its underside, the shell as smooth as his own fingernails. He thought of keeping the struggling land turtle, holding it so the ugly curved beak could not reach his hand, for if it bit, it would not turn loose until it thundered. Then he decided against keeping it. There would not be time to take care of it during the bustle and demands of the auction.

At the first bridge he dropped off the wagon to put the terrapin near water. And when he looked over the wooden railing, he saw the dappled trout, which made him forget his first catch. He yelled at Clint, who drew the wagon up in the shade of a water oak across the bridge.

"It's a great big trout, Papa," he called.

Rolling up his pant legs, Joedel plunged down the embankment, wading toward the creosoted pilings. The foot-long trout had become trapped in a shallow pool, flailing the water, now and then leaping desperately. Speaking to the fish softly, the boy stooped, his bare feet edging forward in the slimy water. A smile on his face, his fingers spread, he struck with the quickness of a rooster after a June bug.

"I got him, Papa!" Joedel cried. "Come see what a big whopper." He waded from the shallow brackish water, holding the trout triumphantly. The thrashing tail beat against his chest, wetting his blue work shirt and filling his nostrils with fish smell.

Just then, downstream and close by, a shotgun went off. Both barrels exploded at once, and the boy heard the scattered shot riddle the leaves above the wooden bridge. A few leaves drifted down into the old mill pond.

"You crazy bastard!" his father yelled, enraged. Then Joedel heard him wrestling with the panicky mules. "Whoa, there. Hold up, I say. Whoa, goddamn your hides!"

Quickly the boy ran a string through the gills of the squirming trout, tying it to a hairy root so it could swim around in the deep black water. Then he scrambled on hands and knees up the steep fishermen's path to the bridge.

Clint had quieted the team, though his face was red with exertion and rage. He yanked their heads up high, the reins gripped in his strong hands. Once again his father shouted a stream of abuse at the hunter who had shot so close by. There was no reply, only his curses echoing from the still swamp and a dog barking across the river.

"You reckon that man might've meant——" Joedel

thought of their poisoned well and the scrawled message with three K's at the bottom.

Clint did not answer. "Git on," he said, "if you're going to market." He spat over the wheel, then spoke to the mules, whose ears were still stiff with alertness, their bits blood-flecked.

As the wagon rolled past, Joedel leaped on. Looking back, he saw that the terrapin had disappeared into the dusty weeds. Soon they were out of the cool shadows and the river came in sight.

But he could not dismiss the blast of the shotgun. If his father had not been on the wagon, their tobacco would now be lost in the Cape Fear River, maybe both runaway mules drowned.

"Some fool hunter," his father said finally. "Ought to be horsewhipped within an inch of his life, then turned in for hunting out of season."

At the landing, there was another delay. Clint Shaw held the team up as the humpbacked ferryman pulled the narrow ferry across the river, heaving against the thick cable.

Joedel could not sit still. He slid off the wagon and threw a pebble at a kingfisher. Birds in the mossy trees were noisy now, sending up their morning songs as the vapor on the river lifted. The boy thought the man-powered ferry would never arrive. Pretending not to look at it, he stood on the bank above a rotted skiff, filling his lungs with the scent of the river, tossing pebbles at cattails. Upstream the trees bent over the river as if they were shaggy mules leaning to drink.

Close to the dead cypress was their secret fishing place. His father had found it the first summer when they borrowed Mr. Sam's skiff, a deep shady place where wide perch and silvery shiners bedded in a tangle of stumps and fallen limbs. They had caught a long string of fish and Joedel ran all the way home to show Maddie his six-pound jack.

Fishing there late in the evenings, Joedel sensed his father's unspoken contentment. While watching the cork in the murky water, the boy saw the worry lines soften in his father's face. Sometimes he would tear off a chew of Hoover tobacco and smile for no reason at his son. Or tease him for fouling his line or snagging only a finger-sized shiner. More than once he let his tattooed arm fall across Joedel's shoulder and stay there, staring contentedly at his bobbing cork, never speaking a word.

After what seemed an endless wait, his father guided the skittish mules down the thick-timbered ramp, talking to them quietly. As the Negro ferryman lifted the heavy chain in place, Joedel chocked the two front wheels.

"That's right. We don't want our weed dumped in this muddy river. Not after all the trouble it's been to us."

The Negro grunted. "It is hellacious to raise, ain't it?"

"By God, it takes thirteen months to the year to raise that infernal crop."

"I chocked them good, Papa."

Then the humpbacked ferryman was straining at the sloping cable, and they were slowly leaving the north bank behind them. As always, Joedel stood with a hand on a wheel spoke, looking downstream, past the fertilizer plant, where the river curved gently toward Wilmington and the Atlantic Ocean. He had been to Wilmington one Fourth of July and now he thought of the high silver bridge that curved across the marsh and river, leading to the city. What would it be like, living in a great city like that?

It felt good to have the heavy timbers beneath him, to feel the rise and fall of the clay-tinted waters. A white heron flew up and he watched it veer, then fly down river. A heron in Cape Fear County was as rare as a trout in a fishing hole, so the boy watched until it had disappeared beyond the tall cypresses, where their trotline was set in the mouth of a creek.

Then the ferryman's shanty on stilts and the gray frame houses drew near, and the ferry was coasting toward the south landing and Sam Eller's sprawling, advertisement-laden general store.

VIII

As the narrow ferry scrunched into the landing, Joedel put his shoes and socks back on, then slid off the bale of hay, easing the strain on the mules. He pushed as the wagon groaned up the steep embankment, turning to smile at the sweating Negro ferryman.

At Sam Eller's store, Clint spoke to the mules, steering them past the yellow gas pump to the watering trough and gooseneck pump. He stopped, as Joedel knew he would.

As eager as he was to reach Clayton, the boy was glad to stop at the general store. Dilapidated and leaning, it was the only remaining store in Ellers Bend and his favorite store in Cape Fear County. Except for the rusty barred windows, much of the front was covered with ads for Tuberose Snuff, soft drinks, and patent remedies. There were crates of soft drink bottles piled helter-skelter beside the kerosene drum on the wide porch.

He followed Clint up the steps, already sensing what he had stopped to buy: a plug of Red Apple tobacco. It was opening day, and it would not be fitting to go to market with a wedge of homemade Hoover tobacco in his hip pocket, yellow wrappers pressed between bricks and flavored with molasses. No, it was a time to splurge, to be extravagant and casually take a store-bought plug out and offer it around to farmers sitting on barrows under the skylights, men who rolled their own cigarettes from sacks of Bull Durham.

The store was empty except for the stout gray-haired storekeeper and his tabby tom behind the counter. He had opened up early because of the auction and was standing behind the counter cleaning an ear with a matchstick, a Dr. Pepper open by the jar of pigs' feet.

"It's gonna be another scorcher," Sam Eller called. "You fellows come in and set a spell." He mentioned that the radio announcer had predicted rain in Waccamaw County.

On the radio now a man was singing:

"Potatoes are cheaper
Tomatoes are cheaper.
Now's the time to fall in love."

While his father asked for the plug of chewing tobacco, Joedel spoke, smiling. He liked Mr. Sam almost as much as he did Cap'n Jim, his older brother. The storekeeper was friendly, with a collection of tales and the leisure to tell them. He had been off to the state university a year and had been a railroad man and traveled as far away as Canada. He teased Joedel about being a "heathen Injun" and saved Indian-head pennies for him and lent him magazines and a few musty books from his assorted collection of mysteries, Jack London, Sir Walter Scott and Zane Grey. Behind the store, he raised pheasants in wire cages, banding them before setting them free.

The boy sat on a fifty-pound salt lick, resting his back against the worn counter next to the smelly fertilizer room by the river. His father and Mr. Sam were talking in early-morning voices. He shifted his tennis shoes on the floor, only half-hearing the gray-haired storekeeper's high-pitched voice as he quarreled about the low price of tobacco.

"What's that radio say about prices in South Carolina, Mr. Sam?"

"Ten, twelve cents." The old storekeeper waved his blunt hand impatiently, his voice rising. "You'll be lucky to get twelve cents for your best grade. I'll be dinged if you won't."

Like his older brother, Mr. Sam was short, no taller than Joedel, but he was stocky and pale, with round sloping shoulders and an incipient paunch. His rimless glasses habitually slid down over his porous red nose. He favored Mr. Jim only in his shrewd blue eyes and the prominent Eller nose. His hands were not liver-splotched but sometimes they trembled as though with palsy.

"An enduring shame," Clint said.

"It's worse than that, by jingoes. It's nothing more than pure stealing the labor off of the poor man. You don't note the rich muckety-mucks losing any weight, or sleep neither, do you now, depression or no depression?"

"You spoke the truth that time."

Joedel tuned them out, settling comfortably on the hard block of salt. He looked at the shiny steel traps and lanterns hanging above the spidery chaotic shelves behind the querulous storekeeper, then at the little post-office window by the door, listening to the cheeps of a shipment of yellow biddies that Mr. Sam had kept overnight.

On the bulletin board were pictures of three wanted men with rewards for their capture. One of them looked like Bruno Hauptmann, who was waiting to be electrocuted in New Jersey. Maybe he and Shag Squires could luck up on one of the wanted men and turn him over to Sheriff Slade. Maybe even John Dillinger or "Baby Face" Nelson. . . . If they got the reward, he would give part of his share to his father to make a payment on the bottom acres Cap'n Jim had promised to sell. Then he might become better tempered and less stingy and Maddie could have her curtains and a new tablecloth. That way, she might become reconciled to the farm and the move away from the cotton mill.

Now his mind abandoned the men of violence and Joe-

del smiled contentedly. Next to his own room at home or the
tobacco barn shelter at night, he enjoyed most being in Mr.
Sam's cluttered and smelly store. Maybe he liked it best of all:
the odor of the round yellow cheese, new blue overalls hanging
from a stretched rope, open boxes of johnnycakes and ginger-
snaps—all mixed in with the smell of chicken starter and laying
mash and molasses. And snuff spit and tobacco juice in the sand-
filled tub under the black wood-burning heater, the cold water
beads on the drink cooler and the steady hum of the storekeeper's Tornado fan behind the left counter. There were fly-
specked ads everywhere for Crazy Water Crystals, 666, and
Red Apple tobacco. He even relished the watery blue paper in
a saucer with the dead flies on it.

All of Joedel's memories of the store were pleasant, except for vaccination days when the lean hairy-armed man
jabbed his coon dog with a big needle, the frightened hound
trembling in the boy's arms. Or when he had to charge the few
groceries his mother sent him for on the rare times when she
ran out before Saturday afternoon. He always hated to say,
"You put that on the book, Mr. Sam?" Dreading that moment
more than anything, he could never look into Sam Eller's eyes,
but took the occasion to twist the neck of the brown paper sack
or stare at the roll of silver link chain or up the stairs, where the
few cured furs were stored and hams and middlings hung on
rusty wires.

To be sure, the genial storekeeper always pulled out his
thick blue-lined ledger cheerfully enough and scribbled in it,
almost illegibly, the price of a pound of coffee or grits or a can
of mackerel or, during canning season, a dozen Mason jars. And
sometimes when Joedel got home he would find candy in the
sack: a few silver bells or two penny jawbreakers.

He much preferred to bring eggs to swap or the soft
drink bottles he found on the shoulders of the new Wilmington
highway, for which he received a penny each in trade. Some
weeks he and his friend Shag found as many as a dozen bottles,
Grapettes and Nehis. Then there would be candy to take home

to his mother and baby sister. It gave him a warm feeling, watching Sissie peel the paper away from the Mary Janes, her eyes as solemn as if she were at a tent revival meeting.

But, of course, the annual dog vaccination days and the bashful misgivings about charging the small sacks of groceries were not enough to cancel out or even mitigate the abiding pleasant memories of the store at the ferry landing. Especially when he and his father walked there on cold winter nights. When they listened to the heavyweight fights on the staticky radio or, hushed and solemn, to President Roosevelt's talks, the boy could feel hope surging in the tired overalled man, as strong and palpable as the scent of sassafras. Hope that seemed warm enough to melt the six-inch icicles from the eaves.

At such times, the store became a totally masculine world, given over to rawboned, sunburned farmers, guano and sawmill workers, crosstie cutters and Negro sharecroppers. The sharecroppers did not do much trading, but Mr. Sam welcomed them all, white and black, for he was more than ever lonely since his wife had died and there was only a young mulatto girl who came once a week to clean the untidy rooms behind the store. He was a friendly, loquacious man, and he needed the comfort of talk more than the dimes and quarters spent after dark. Besides, he had a good farm which added to his income considerably—in spite of his incessant feuds with tenants who changed annually.

Joedel remembered best the nights when the talk turned to him, when his father had taken a drink from the storekeeper's fruit jar and was egged on by Mr. Sam to boast about his only son.

"Joedel's a big help to you now, ain't he, Clinton?"

The boy would look down at his half-soled work shoes, bashful.

"I couldn't farm a lick without him." Then Clint would go on to say how he could lay off the straightest rows of any boy in Ellers Bend. To begin with his father let him lay off the rows only in the backfields and they were, at first, crooked enough. But ever since he'd turned twelve, he had laid off rows by the road, where every passerby could see how straight the stands of corn or soybeans were. He always plowed the slowest of the government mules, keeping the white strip of cloth on the pole sighted between her stiff ears. In the end, since he had more patience than his father, his rows were as straight as if they were marked with a chalked string, far straighter than Clint's.

Or again: "Look at that boy shoot up, Mistuh Clint. He grows like a weed. He's gonna be as big as Max Baer, I declare he is now."

"And as strong as that Red Indian Liniment yonder."

"Shooting up like he is, he must put fertilizer in them gunboats there."

"Yeah," Clint would say, "he's gonna have a good understanding. It's a fact."

Mr. Sam would persist. "Jim says he's a good sled boy. Says he's the best sled boy he's got now—and you know he ain't one to brag on anybody. It ain't in his nature."

Doll Boney had said, "You be's a man when you quits driving a sled and makes a cropper."

But of course Shag Squires claimed you weren't a man until you'd been with a woman, the way he'd been with the colored girl in the cotton shed and bragged about how her pomaded hair had left a greasy spot on his shirt.

Now Joedel waited until his father and Mr. Sam had finished discussing the prices of tobacco on the South Carolina market and the storekeeper had gone into his customary tirade against the big companies who controlled prices, keeping them low in spite of the rising economy since President Roosevelt moved into the White House.

"I tell you Roosevelt's going to have to build a fire under some of them scoundrels. You mark my words."

There was a moment of gray silence and Joedel asked, "Any mail come for me yesterday, Mr. Sam?" He stared at the three pictures tacked near the little post-office window.

"Nope, not a scratch." The storekeeper peered owlishly at the boy over the top of his dusty glasses. "Clinton, the way that yearling's always after me about the mail, I'll be dinged if I don't believe he's expecting a sugar report from some little gal or other. Don't you reckon he's consorting with some little heifer over yonder at Clayton we don't know about? It wouldn't surprise me at all. That boy's close, he don't tell all he knows."

"He's getting mighty big for his britches," his father said. "It won't be long before he's smelling around the gals, I reckon." Clint said it was the usual way. "You go to the trouble and expense of raising a boy up, then when he's old enough to be some help, why you can't depend on him. He's more than likely traipsing off after some little split-tail."

"You better leave 'em be for a while yet, young buck." Mr. Sam winked at Clinton and laughed his funny snuffling laugh. "I declare now. Just look at the way he's slicked up, hair combed and all. Shoes on, bless me, and it not Sunday, even wearing socks. Why, they won't even know there at Clayton he's a heathen Injun, he's so decked out in clean dungarees and folderols."

Secretly pleased, Joedel listened to their teasing, though the tone of his father's voice was more than half-serious. It was Mr. Sam's habit to tease him about the girls, ever since he'd seen him bashfully walking home from the Baptist Church with Opal Mears.

But Mr. Sam knew as well as Joedel that it was no girl's letter he was expecting. He was anxious to hear from *The Progressive Farmer*. He had entered the magazine's essay contest for young readers and daily looked forward to hearing from the editorial office in Texas. Once he had dreamed of receiving the five-dollar check for the best essay on "My Favorite Season," but it had not come. The money would have been more than enough to buy the baseball mitt his heart was set on.

Joedel almost always entered the monthly contests. Once he had given up in despair, but that very month he read that a 4-H boy in Waccamaw County had won, a fourteen-year

old boy from Ammons. After that he had gone back to tearing
out the contest page of Mr. Sam's magazine and writing his ag-
onizingly composed essay in ink on rough tablet paper. He had
never heard a word from the stony-hearted editors in Dallas,
yet he continued to ponder their uninspired topics, posting his
essays with high hopes:

"My Most Frightening Experience" (the time he had
reached blindly into the hen's nest and grabbed hold of a big
chicken snake); "My Worst Mistake" (the time he had run off,
chasing a June bug with a piece of twine tied to its leg. He was
supposed to be tending to Sissie and when he returned she had
climbed up on the well curb); "My Most Exciting Experience"
(the first time he'd gone to the tobacco market with Cap'n Jim
and his father. They had journeyed the fourteen miles to
Brownsville and had spent the night at the warehouse. Joedel
had slept under the stars in the truck body, the smelly tarpaulin
for a mattress).

Now his father looked at him, his jaw bulging with the
cut of tobacco. "We got to hit the road."

Joedel stood up.

"You all don't rush off," Mr. Sam said.

"Got to. The Cap'n'll be raising cane if we're late."

"Well, hold up a minute."

All of a sudden, Mr. Sam looked at Clint, his round face
serious, questioning. "What was the commotion about while
ago?"

"What's that now?"

"I mean the shooting and all. I heard somebody mortally
cussing a blue streak."

Clint explained that it was only an accident. "Come to
think of it, I reckon whoever it was did figure I'd left the mules
untended when Joedel called me."

Mr. Sam lowered his voice. "Clinton, you be careful. I
heard some talk."

"What kind of talk, Mr. Sam?"

"Just talk, maybe just trifling talk that won't amount to a hill of beans."

His father had quit chewing. "What did you hear?"

"Well, they know about your plans. Some of them rough rednecks know about your and Jim's agreement about the land, and they're dead set against you buying any dirt in Ellers Bend."

His father turned away. "That's just between me and Mr. Jim. It's not anybody else's business."

"I know that, man. It's exactly what I told them when they came to see me. I wouldn't've mentioned it, only I heard the shot and you cussing thataway."

To change the subject, Mr. Sam decided to have a look at the tobacco loaded on the wagon. Joedel was pleased, for he knew Mr. Sam would compare their crop with that of his Negro tenants, who were notoriously shiftless. Unlike his older brother, the storekeeper could never manage his workers, and they took advantage of him.

Joedel followed Mr. Sam down the sagging porch steps and out to the wagon, catching the faint smell of whiskey on his rumpled clothes. His khaki trousers were baggy, held up by wide red suspenders, which habitually had to be adjusted on his sloping shoulders. Clint bit off a fresh chew from the plug of Red Apple tobacco, squinting at the sun as a noisy flock of grackles squabbled up toward the mustard-yellow depot.

The storekeeper spit snuff juice on the wheel rim, like a splotch of brown gravy, then fumbled under the quilt and worked loose a hank, beating it on his right knee.

"This here your best grade?"

"Second," Clint said, suppressing a grin.

Mr. Sam clucked, beat the bundle again until the pressed leaves fell apart. Then he thrust his red nose into the pliant tobacco, his bifocals suddenly coated with dust as fine as snuff.

"That's the pure money-weed you got there, man. It sure-God ought to sell, if anything sells good in this hell-heated world."

Clint Shaw obviously relished this praise. "It did cure out right pretty, Mr. Sam. But it's light, got no body to it since the hail took the main stalk, you know. But I can't complain." He climbed up behind the restive mules.

"I reckon not. I'd settle for light weight, with the pretty color you got. By jingoes, I wish my crowd would cure out one barn like yours there, just one little cropping. And not go gallivanting off or get drunk and scorch it or turn it red as a baboon's butt."

The storekeeper put the hank back, folding the quilt down and smoothing it carefully. Turning away, he caught Clint's eye and winked.

"Hold on here. Where's Joedel's weed now? I want to see what that young scamp's gonna put on the floor his first time out. Don't you go and disgrace us in Clayton, boy."

Joedel pointed to the sheet-wrapped pile on top of the load, his father explaining how he took no risk but was keeping the damaged lot separate, not even letting it touch his good tobacco. "They smell any rot on my good tobacco, then look out, it'll be too wet to plow."

Joedel watched as the old man fished out a hank, repeating the same ritual, beating it loose on his right knee. He blew his nose loudly, then plunged his face into the tobacco.

The boy's dark eyes narrowed. As he watched the sunlight on the lemon-colored leaves, he was thinking: This is it, now. If he smells the rotten scent, it will go for next to nothing and there won't be any baseball mitt. I might even have to fetch it back home and throw it in the hog lot, with everybody in Ellers Bend learning how I struck out my first time at the auction. Already he could envision Shag Squires' lips drawn back from his horse teeth.

Mr. Sam lowered the sample hank, squinting at Joedel, a smile flickering on his lips.

Clint Shaw spoke first. "What you think, Mr. Sam?"

The gray-haired storekeeper slipped the bundle back in place, patting the tobacco lightly. "By jingoes, Clint, there's no thinking two ways about it. That weed's not rotten, it's not about to be damaged—yet. All I could smell was a touch of fennel where he laid it out in the dew to bring it in order.

"Not to mention the snuff. Hell-fire, that yearling damn near bought me out of Sweet Society snuff to disguise that one basket of primers. I declare unto you, all I could smell now was green fennel and Sweet Society snuff."

Mr. Sam looked at Joedel, his eyes crinkled. "Tell you what. I'll wager them buyers don't notice a thing, boy. I'll just bet you now. If they find it out on you, you don't owe me one cent for all the snuff you bought on credit. They do, you'll have to cough up the fifty cents. Is that a bet?"

"Well," Joedel said. He did not know if Mr. Sam was serious or not.

He glanced at his father, whose smile told him nothing. But he knew Mr. Sam was in earnest when he reached out and shook his hand, like two men who had wagered high stakes.

Joedel climbed on the wagon and sat on the bale of hay. "I worked mighty hard on that little dab of tobacco, me and Mama."

Maddie had helped him tie it at night by lantern light, sneaking limp tie leaves from Clint's best grade.

"Well, you don't have to worry about the buyers. Just you look out for pinhookers, boy. They're cunning rogues, with noses like them prison camp bloodhounds over yonder at Silver Lake."

"Much obliged, Mr. Sam," Clint said. "We gonna stop off and pay you something on our furnish on the way back."

"No hurry. No big rush at all."

His father spoke to the white mules and the wagon creaked slowly past the rusty pump, then onto the clay road.

Mr. Sam called after them. "That tobacco's not rotten. It's like a woman that's just a leetle bit pregnant. Ain't nothing showing up—yet." He slapped his knee and walked back up the steps.

Yes, Joedel thought, by the time something shows, it'll be long gone and too late. The tobacco will be somewhere in storage or a drying plant, maybe. And I'll have the check and it all spent.

But then he frowned: You better not count your biddies until they're hatched. He waved at Mr. Sam as he stooped to scratch his cat's ear.

THE TEAM OF WHITE MULES WAS EAGER TO resume their journey. Without a word from Clint Shaw, they fell into a fast gait, their ears stiff and their heads working like triphammers. Soon they had passed the scaling frame houses, the boarded-up drygoods store and old blacksmith shop, then the abandoned cotton gin.

The boy turned to look at Mr. Sam Eller's sawmill and the bark-strewn, weedy lumber yard. The mill had been closed now for two years: no one had money to buy lumber any more. The mountainous sawdust pile had lost its fresh odor, turning a dull red, its warped cross slanting in the wind. The few piles of hacked lumber were weathered and gray. At the edge of the mill yard he noticed a workman's glove, palm up, a briar growing between its fingers.

When they rattled across the single track at the mustard-colored depot, Joedel glanced up the Seaboard tracks toward the swamps and Clayton. He saw a tramp resting in the shade of the huge water tank. A greasy sack in one hand, the man was rolling a cigarette with the other, a shapeless cap hiding his face.

Joedel thought of the few hungry men who had come to beg since they moved from Cottonmill Hill. His mother always spared them something to eat, no matter how little they had themselves.

She half grumbled to Clint, "There's always folks worse off than us, seems like."

A little feist ran out to snap at the rear wheel, and Joedel kicked at it, yelling, "Get! You better get now, Blackie."

The dog ran behind a pile of crossties stacked near the railroad siding. Joedel cupped his eyes. He squinted into the sun at the pile of oak crossties. In the harsh sunlight they lay flat and clean, as neat as picked bones.

For a few minutes he read the paper he'd picked up on the store porch. The news was almost all bad. The Italians were massing their troops in Abyssinia and in Berlin a woman dating a Jew had her hair shaved off and her head tarred. In America Harry Hopkins had cut the relief rolls so farmers could get their crops harvested. Doris Duke had been married in Hong Kong and her husband announced that he was returning to New York to set Roosevelt straight on how to treat the rich.

Joedel wrapped the paper around the greasy sack that held their dinner, brushing a fly away. He did not want the news of a remote world to cast a pall over the market day at Clayton.

"Just look at that, would you?"

Joedel stood up and stared over the Star of Bethlehem quilt.

He had never seen such traffic on the highway—trucks, cars and wagons. The procession toward the warehouses reminded him of a picture he'd seen of the Okies going to California. Every type of vehicle had been drafted to haul the golden harvest to the auction. Tobacco was piled in rumble seats, in horse-drawn smooth-running Hoover carts, rickety trailers pulled by Model A's. The boy even saw a white-haired Negro hauling a few pounds in the foot of a black-topped buggy and, later, a Whippet running with two wheels on the rims.

All the traffic was flowing toward Clayton, though some of the farmers would not stop there. They would continue to Lumberton or turn south to Brownsville, market towns large enough to warrant two sets of buyers. All winter the farmers had gone without cash income; now they urged their old cars and emaciated mules toward the warehouses, an opening-day excitement on their lean faces.

Joedel said, "It's good we got our space reserved, ain't it, Papa?" Some of the farmers would spend two days in town, sleeping on the warehouse floor, before they could sell their tobacco and return home to sort and tie the next cropping.

Clint grunted and maneuvered the team and wagon onto the Wilmington highway, turning away from the sun. The mules fell into a steady trot, their hoofs loud on the cement. Joedel sat on the baled hay, observing how tractor spikes had bitten into the cement crossing on the road to Ellers Bend. Already he saw scattered tobacco leaves along the shoulders of the new highway, lemon leaves among the yellow of wild marigolds. Later the rain-beaten leaves would decay and disappear, followed by the litter of cotton lint in November.

They had not gone more than a mile, with the noisy traffic rushing past them, when the sun went behind some gray clouds. Suddenly, a breeze arose and the clouds turned darker, as if churned by dark winds. Joedel recalled what the weatherman had said on Mr. Sam's radio about rain in Waccamaw County.

Clint twisted around, his eyes alarmed. "Them quilts covering everything?"

Joedel nodded. As he smoothed out the giant star, a few drops splashed against his forehead and into his eyes. The boy held his palms out to test the rain. A car blew impatiently and Clint pulled the wagon so far to the right that two wheels dropped to the rough shoulder, jolting the boy until he almost sat in their dinner.

Now the big drops fell harder, and Joedel thought of his mother's favorite quilt. Already the six-pointed stars were dotted with wet splotches.

Cursing, Clint Shaw lashed at the mules with the plow

lines. The startled team lurched forward and the loaded wagon lumbered at a faster pace. Joedel felt the rhythm change as the white mules broke into a trot together, Clint standing on the wagon tongue and cutting their damp flanks with the lines. "Git up, you hammerheaded sons-of-bitches!"

He did not understand how his father could be so cruel.

Just then the rain came in a burst and a Mack truck passed them, handwipers working. A man in a striped railroad cap stuck his head out of the window and yelled, "Git a truck," laughing idiotically.

Clint Shaw shook his fist and hurled curses after the vanishing joker.

The wagons ahead of them on the highway were covered safely with tarpaulins, but even so the drivers were lashing furiously at their teams.

Then Joedel realized that Clint was cursing him. His face had twisted around. "Get off, goddam it, I said!" He was slapping the tobacco with a flattened hand.

Joedel jumped off the tailgate. Running behind the wagon, he saw the mules shift into an awkward lope. The boy kept up easily, his arms drawn up to his chest, his black hair plastered to his skull by the driving rain.

The dark clouds would soon blow over toward Wilmington, but his father had not glanced at the sky. Pelted by the shower, he raged at the nervous mules, beating them furiously.

Suddenly, Joedel saw him jerk viciously at the reins. The heavy wagon plunged off the new hard surface, then leaned dangerously as Clint whipped the mules up the embankment. The team and wagon lurched under the open shelter of Mr. Sam Eller's tobacco barn, smashing off the wooden supports for tobacco crates.

Joedel had fallen behind; now he heard his father call to him to get out of the rain. When he clambered up the clay embankment, his shoes soggy, Clint was already reaching his hand under the pulled-back quilts, his narrowed eyes searching.

Joedel walked slowly under the open shelter, the rain

pelting steadily on the tin roof. He ran his fingers through his coarse, wet hair, leaning on a stringer to catch his breath.

He looked at his father.

"It ain't hurt none, no more than damp." Another mile or so, Clint said, and the whole sides and top would have been soaked. "It would be as worthless as them—as them sticks of yours might be." He stretched the quilts back in place, brushing the rain off with his cupped hands.

Joedel did not inspect his tobacco wrapped in the sack sheet. He sat in the open barn door, thinking of his father's cruelty, the blood-flecked bits in the mouths of the mules. How could he beat the mules so fiercely?

When he looked up, Clint Shaw was stroking the nose of Rhodie, the off mule. His eyes were shiny and he spoke with a tight smile. "By God, we made it, didn't we, Rhodie? We made it, old gal." Then he added, "Looks like we have to go through hell and high water to get this cussed weed to market. Then more than likely the buyers will steal it."

He unwired the bale of hay and gave each mule a small block of dry hay. They shook the rain off their clipped manes and began eating, stomping under the shelter of the tarpapered barn. Clint began repairing the crate support, hammering the nails back in with a brick.

The boy stood up then. He climbed on the spokes and inspected his sheet of tobacco. Only a few leaves were wet on top. He pulled them from the tight hanks and threw them away, tying the sheet back up, his nose quivering with the smell of the wet mules and damp tobacco and the slimy odor of the trout on his shirt.

When he glanced across the stringers, he saw that Shadrach and Mr. Eller had driven up in the truck and parked off the road below them. The Negro sharecropper was driving, Mr. Jim beside him in his seersucker suit and white Panama hat. In the back, leaning on the wet tarpaulin, were Booster and two other Negro sharecroppers, their overalls soaking wet.

Cap'n Jim rolled down the window. "You all all right?"

"We're just fine," Joedel called. "It didn't get wet none—not a leaf."

"We had room aplenty for your tobacco."

Clint replied brusquely, "Go ahead on. You all don't need to worry about us."

Shad leaned around Mr. Jim. "You want us to come back for your baccer, Mistuh Clint?" He looked anxiously up the clay embankment, the whites of his eyes shining.

"It's blowing over now," the boy said. He could not keep silent, for he knew how his father's pride was hurt, how he must be seething.

"Go ahead on, I say. You all don't need to concern yourself about us." Clint Shaw's face was lined with fury.

Shadrach and Mr. Eller talked among themselves. Then the old man called weakly, "It's all but stopped now. But you all take care. I'll send Shad and Booster back if there's another shower."

"We'll save your space, Mistuh Clint."

"You do that thing." Clint Shaw looked away from the men in the cab.

Then the truck was gone, pulling out in the traffic, which was becoming infrequent now.

"Taking their trashy mess in style, while my good tobacco gets wet in them raggedy quilts."

Joedel turned away from his father's wrath. Stooping, he stepped in the open door of the curing barn. It was a new barn with silvery flues and two-by-four tier poles instead of rough logs. The day before, it had been filled with strung tobacco, and the rank gummy leaves were wilting, already yellowing, waiting for the furnace to be fired.

But before he could sit down, his father said, "It's done blowed over." The storm had passed swiftly, and with it Clint's anger. "Get on board, boy."

ON THE ROAD AGAIN, THEY SAW HOW THE TRAFFIC had dwindled. His father sat stiffly, the new straw hat lost in the rain, urging the mules into a trot. Joedel observed how he concentrated on handling the team, not turning his head. Ordinarily he would be studying the crops on both sides of the highway, the tobacco harvested halfway up the stalk, the rye and peanuts and maturing cotton. For Clint Shaw judged a man's character by how clean his fields were, by the growth on his ditchbanks and the wild mustard in his pasture. He had learned from his association with Mr. Jim Eller that it was an infallible way of sizing up a man.

As they entered the first stretch of swamp, they came upon a chain gang, a dozen Negroes wading knee deep in stagnant water. Their long bright bush hooks flashed in the sun as they cleared the right-of-way. The boy stared at their black-and-white-striped prison garb, glancing away from the shackled legs of the three men on the road shoulder. Their stripes were vertical and it meant that they were long-termers, men who had killed or raped or robbed. Never breaking the rhythm of their hacking, they all turned to look at the copper-skinned boy on the wagon, regarding him almost shyly. They were singing, keeping time with their hawk-billed blades, lifting a song in the haze of mosquitoes and gnats, moving jerkily in the evil-smelling water. They were singing under the shadow of the white guard's shotgun, drowning out the clink of their chains.

As the two-horse wagon neared the chain gang, the mulatto water boy stood up, smiling obsequiously. He was not much older, and no taller, than Joedel. As the wagon rattled by, suddenly the young prisoner stuck a leather wallet under Joedel's nose. His legs were not chained, and he ran behind the wagon, holding out the wallet, begging Joedel to buy it.

"Only fifty cent, mister. Only fifty cent, please."

Feeling shamed, Joedel shook his head and the prisoner gave up, a mournful expression on his yellow face. Joedel knew that it was a look that would haunt him the whole market day, and beyond. He was relieved when the truck and fat guard blocked his view of the chained black convicts.

All this time Clint Shaw sat woodenly, looking neither to the right nor left, ignoring the wave of the potbellied man cradling the shotgun.

Now the team's hoofs were echoing off the trees which pushed up from the swamps, stretching back to the Seaboard Railway and the river. For three years Joedel had ridden the orange school bus over the highway. Once he had walked home when the bus driver left him dawdling on the baseball diamond. The road was rich in associations for him.

Where the road curved Joedel noted the high clay embankment. He turned to look at the deep holes dug in the blood-red earth. Those pits were made by the clay eaters. He had seen the Negroes cramming the damp clay into paper sacks, taking it home furtively. But he had never seen them eat any in public. It did not seem right to him, eating the earth itself. It was like urinating on it until the salt killed the ground and nothing more would grow on it.

When he spoke of this to Maddie, she only grunted, "Niggers." He could not comprehend her harshness.

Now they rounded the last curve before the narrow white bridge by Indigo Pond. It was a sharp curve, dangerous. Here was where the silver oil tanker had turned over, spilling its gasoline in the little clay ditch. Everyone in Ellers Bend had turned out with galvanized tubs and barrels, hauling away the oil in wagons and tobacco slides, ignoring the curses of the unhurt driver.

Two years ago in the same shallow ditch he had seen his first dead person other than his Indian grandmother in her wooden casket at Pembroke. There had been a wreck, a black Cadillac had hit a mule and wagon. When Joedel and Clint passed in their cart, they saw the dead mule, stiff-legged, on the shoulder of the road. Then when Joedel summoned his courage to look into the ditch, between the somber overalled farmers he glimpsed the dead body of Ariel Lacey. How small he looks in the ditch, he thought. Not like a grown man, but more like a boy his own age. There was a reddish smear on the mulatto's mustache, the color of his skin the same as Joedel's.

That night in his room, he lay awake and listened to the keening Negroes as they walked up the clay road. He stared into the darkness. "His shoes were untied," he said aloud to Jean Harlow, drifting into a broken sleep.

Passing the drainage ditch, Joedel turned his back on it, twisting on his knees to look at the white cement bridge and, in the distance, the round silver water tower of Clayton.

The road was no longer wet and steamy from the sudden shower. Joedel grew tired of waving at the cars and trucks that passed. He lost count of the different models, though he remembered the Cord and Terraplane and the old Model T with the tobacco piled on the car top.

Once he jumped off to snatch up a Grapette bottle in the wild marigolds. Later he thought he glimpsed one of Mr. Sam's pheasants in the dark woods. Bored, he slipped from the wagon and snatched a wad of tar from the road. He began to chew it like chewing gum, but it was gritty and strong and he spit it out, sprinting to catch up with the rattling wagon.

The mules were trotting at a fast pace. His father had

shucked off his denim coat again, and Joedel saw the white X
where his overall suspenders crossed, where the sweat stains
were spreading on his blue work shirt.

Now an idea took hold of him: he would run the last
three miles to Clayton. He would run so that he could boast to
Shag Squires how he'd run almost the whole way to the market.
Keeping behind the loaded wagon, Joedel ran smoothly, listening to the clatter of the trotting hoofs, the musical jingle of the
chains. He swung his arms and lengthened his stride, falling
into an easy rhythm. He kept his head low so Clint could not
see him.

But after a mile his legs began to ache and a blister
formed on his heel. The notion did not seem so attractive to
him, but he stuck to it stubbornly. Finally, he held to the tailgate, letting the mules pull him forward. This was cheating, he
knew, but still it was his own legs that were devouring the last
miles to Clayton. Finally, he gave up and crawled back on the
wagon. Merely having a basket of his own tobacco was, in a
way, a victory over Shag Squires.

When they came out of the swamps, Clint turned off the
highway to avoid traffic, heading toward the river on a bumpy
dirt road that caused the wagon to rise and dip sharply, creaking in protest. Joedel let his legs dangle, while his calf muscles
jerked in little spasms. On his right were the swamps, giving
way to pine thickets, on his left, cleared fields of cotton and
tobacco and a pasture gone back to fennel and goldenrod, then
a field of orange broom sedge. Behind him he saw a new sign at
the turnoff that said REPENT.

"Repent," he said aloud, wondering again if he should
mark *Damaged* on his sales ticket when they unloaded at the
warehouse. Then he dismissed the thought from his mind.

After a quarter of a mile, his legs stopped trembling and
Joedel stood up, the quilts dry under his hands. Now he could
see Clayton a mile off: the water tower with Class of 34 painted
on it in red, the three-story hotel with the tin-roofed turret and
rusty fire escape, where the tobacco buyers lived and the

wealthy farmers ate dinners served family-style. Beyond the scaling hotel, which leaned to one side like Mr. Sam's store, the boy saw the smokestack of Hester's Lumber Mill. It was taller than the white steeples of the Baptist and Methodist churches needling up from green oaks and elms.

His father snorted, pointing. In the ruined pasture a tent was stretched out in the grass and weeds. "There you are," Clint said. "A hell-fired preacher come to rake up any loose nickels now the market's open again."

Joedel recalled the Baptist minister who was frightened by his father's fierceness after the hailstorm.

But no preacher could be seen, only the rumpled canvas like a deflated balloon, a stack of folded chairs near the deserted Dodge pickup. Near the chairs was a big sign that read REUBEN BONES, EVANGELIST, and under that, MIRACLE CRUSADE.

Next to the meeting ground, the wagon creaked past the town dump, oily smoke coiling up from the center. There was a steep declivity, rain runneled, which sloped to a stagnant pond draining under the railroad trestle into the river. Joedel saw a flock of Negro children, like starlings, picking over the ash heaps and strewn junk.

When the loaded wagon turned west a final time, the boy felt the tiredness drain out of him. Now the mules seemed aware of their journey's end. Their wet flanks seemed to give off steam, their ears alert. The dull thud of their hoofs picked up without a flick of the plow lines from Clint, raising a little cloud of reddish dust, for the sudden shower had missed Clayton.

The boy looked eagerly over their heads at the sun-parched town before him. He could see the long tin warehouses and the yellow river that divided the market town, the rusty bridge that arched over the sluggish river. Already he could hear the snarl of traffic, angry horns, and the shouts of impatient farmers.

"By damn, we'll have to fight our way into the New Deal, it looks like," Clint said.

They were passing the cotton gin, the sun shining on the

corrugated tin roof. When the tobacco warehouses closed, its machinery would hum again, the big pipe sucking up the cotton from the line of loaded trucks and wagons. Then the squat bales of cotton would spill out from the loading ramp and into the weedy lot.

On their left was a drab row of derelict houses decaying toward the river. Joedel looked at their slanted porches and gray-weathered siding. Gingerbread fell away from gables and lathe-turned banisters were missing. There was not a patch of grass in any of the yards.

"Good Lord," the boy exclaimed, "look at that traffic jam." They wouldn't be able to drive around front, blocked by the trucks and wagons on the paved street and narrow crowded bridge. It was like Lake Waccamaw on the Fourth of July.

Then the line of loaded wagons and trucks came to a complete halt, followed by shouts and irritable horns.

"Go up yonder and see what the holdup is," Clint said. "Make haste now." Already his temper was rising.

On the main street leading across the bridge, Joedel saw that the traffic was stalled as far as he could see in both directions. Clayton had been metamorphosed from a somnolent town to a frenzied tobacco center. His nose quivered with the scent of flue-cured tobacco permeating the August air. Bright hanks were scattered in the road with trampled horse manure. Farmers crowded the sidewalks, sample bundles under their sweaty arms.

Before the entrance to the New Deal, a small cricket of a man in a straw boater waved a striped cane, shouting, "Drive in the house, Cap'n. Plenty room left for tomorrow. First sale tomorrow morning."

Beyond the tin warehouse, Joedel saw that the medicine man had set up his canvas booth in front of Cox's mule stables. Only a small knot of farmers stood around, but after the sales the booth would be encircled. Above the maniacal horns Joedel heard a snatch of the medicine man's spiel: "We're all on a trip to the graveyard, folks. Might as well feel good along the way now," his long arm holding up a bottle of miraculous tonic.

The boy remembered the quavering owl that cried near the barn before dawn. Wheeling, he walked down the rutted clay road by the river, not looking at the stalled farmers who waited a chance to pull out into the main street. He knew his father would be angry.

"Hey, Joedel."

It was two of his classmates fishing with cane poles on the riverbank.

He paused for a moment, looking at the town boys, who wore white shirts and knickers that fell loosely halfway to their ankles. His arms hung awkwardly and he became aware of his patched shirt.

"How'd you get to town? You all come in that Hoover cart?"

Shaking his dark head, he started to say he'd ridden in Mr. Eller's truck, but he pulled up short.

"You staying over for the show?"

"What show?"

"The picture show, that's what." There was to be a movie that night, shown by the Chamber of Commerce, between the New Deal and Cox's mule stables. The farmers and townspeople would sit on the grass and watch the free Western.

"They say it's gonna be a Buck Jones or Hoot Gibson."

"You ever seen them in a picture show?"

Joedel shook his head no. He had seen a Rin-Tin-Tin once in a traveling tent show and a Tom Mix and a Ken Maynard, and that was all.

"You don't know what you're missing, boy. Better stay over."

He would like to stay in Clayton and see the free movie, but he knew his father would never waste time on such a trifling thing.

"I've got to get on and unload," Joedel said. But before turning away he told them he had a basket for sale in the auction.

"Hell I reckon. Your own tobacco?"

He could not help noting the change in their eyes, how

their grins dried up. Walking toward the team of lathered mules, he knew that he had grown taller in their eyes. If he had a good sale, he'd be sure to tell his classmates how much his basket of tobacco brought.

Suddenly, there was Booster running down the exit ramp, looking important in his ragged overalls. Waving his arms, he cried, "You all's to come in the back way. Cap'n Jim done cleared it with Mr. Barefoot."

Clint turned the white mules, swearing, and when the back ramp was empty he carefully guided them up the incline. Joedel and Booster walked behind the wagon as Clint threaded his way skillfully toward the high green scales in the center of the New Deal Warehouse.

JOEDEL HAD BEEN TO THE TOBACCO MARKET OVER a dozen times, yet today it was different, almost as if he had never been before. And he knew the reason: Cap'n Jim's gift wrapped in burlap, separated from his father's tobacco. Having his own few pounds to risk on the auction somehow changed things, made opening day an unknown quantity. Even the aromatic odor of the tobacco that rose up now to strike his nostrils seemed sharper; the gold and lemon colors were intensified under the skylights. His scalp prickled as if stuck with a thousand tiny needles.

The New Deal Warehouse was crowded and noisy. Everywhere Joedel looked there were shallow baskets of tobacco filling up the long straight rows. The tin warehouse was stifling hot, and soon everyone was coated with sweat. But the excitement was contagious—the roar of the big trucks, farmers shouting at nervous mules, the floor manager banging his shiny steel hook on the littered floor. A short dark-haired girl was threading her way through the crowd selling sandwiches, followed by a boy with cold drinks in an icy bucket. Near the front ramp, Joedel saw a blind Negro picking a guitar. The beggar sat in a chair singing, but no one heard him above the bustle of the teeming warehouse.

As they were shucking the quilts and damp sack sheets off the tobacco, the tall stranger appeared. Mr. Jim had gone off to inquire about the early sale in the Planters, across the bridge. Joedel had found an unclaimed dolly near the loading pit and rolled it back to the wagon, maneuvering it between the trucks and wagons, skirting the knots of expectant farmers. Shadrach appeared with six latticed crates and dumped them by the starred quilt, causing the nervous mules to jerk their heads up.

Joedel eased the wooden barrow down and looked at the newcomer.

The red-mustached stranger wore a fancy hat with a feather in it, two-toned perforated shoes, and creased blue trousers. He ran his hand over the top layer of tobacco, then unloosened a short-leafed yellow hank. Spreading the leaves, he sniffed them, studying the color with eyes like green scuppernongs flecked with tan. Afterward his close-set eyes settled on Shadrach Gillings, who stood in faded overalls, an empty basket by his side.

"This your wagonload of tobacco?" His voice was imperious, raspy.

"No suh, boss. It belong to Mistuh Shaw there." Shad nodded at Clint, his dark face solemn.

"That a fact?"

The man returned the short hank, running his spidery fingers down the load to the wagon side. Joedel saw him studying Clint covertly across the empty dolly. Not once did the stranger look directly at Clint; his shifty eyes were more on the boy by the wooden dolly.

"Tell you what I'll do," the man commenced, running his long hand over the well-ordered leaves. "I hear the sale's gonna be delayed a good spell, maybe throw you fellas spending the night. Now I know you don't want to waste two whole days hanging around waiting for the auction. Not when you could be home working up your next curing. So I'll just naturally make you a offer for your whole load here."

Shad widened his eyes, but no one spoke. There was a well of silence around them.

The stranger looked shrewdly at Clint Shaw.

"I'm gonna offer you eight cents a pound for the whole lot. You'll save the warehouse charges and the auction fees, not to mention the cost of stopping over."

Joedel saw his father shake his head, frowning.

"All right, nine cents a pound. That's as high as I'll go. Way I figger it, I'm doing you fellas a favor."

He placed a hand on the tobacco, leaning against the wagon. Across the warehouse the floor manager was shouting at a driver who was blocking the entrance.

"Nobody asked you for a favor, Mister." His father kept his voice steady.

"I'm not denying that. But there's one thing you oughta know, Mac." The tall man paused for effect. "Anybody can tell this tobacco's been hit by hail. Ain't that a fact now?"

Nobody answered.

Joedel thought, Somebody must've told him that. He knew what to look for.

"It ain't worth a whole lot, raised like it is off a sucker."

"Then how come you offer nine cents a pound?" Clint bridled.

The stranger shrugged and said he was a friend of every farmer. "Besides, not every buyer can spot a sucker growth like me. I figger to get my investment back, maybe a penny more."

"You a pinhooker?"

The rangy man nodded, smiling a thin-lipped smile. "I do some speculating. Yeah."

"Then get your goddam hand off of my tobacco."

The pinhooker straightened up, his hand dropping to his side. One of the mules blew loudly, clearing its nostrils.

"I don't want it bruised, Mister."

"You heard my final offer."

"I'm gonna make out like I ain't heard nothing, while you sneak along to cheat some other poor bastard out of his hard-earned crop."

The two men looked at one another a moment, and Joedel saw the naked hatred in his father's smoldering eyes.

"You better make yourself scarce now."

Without a word the pinhooker sidled past Shad and Joedel, a fixed smile on his sweaty face, then walked rapidly away.

Joedel watched him until he was lost in the crowd, thinking, He thought we were colored. All the time he thought we were ignorant Negroes and wouldn't know any better than to let him cheat us out of our crop.

Shad dropped the crate on the wooden barrow, smiling. "Hunh. That's one man got hisself told off. He's one white man sure got the word."

Booster added, "I just wish Cap'n Jim was here to hear it."

Clint's anger subsided. "Get up there, Joedel, and hand us that tobacco down."

"Papa, I want to pack my pile on——"

"You heard me, boy," he flared up. "Pass that tobacco on down now."

Joedel looked at Shad, then climbed up on the tailgate and began passing the loaded sticks down.

When they were weighing up and rolling the baskets of tobacco to Row 13, Joedel saw Mr. Eller walking up the front ramp, passing the blind folk singer. He had been over to watch the sale at the Planters Warehouse, and his periwinkle eyes were somber.

The floor manager, a stocky man in sweated khaki, walked over, a steel hook under his arm.

"How much you all putting on the floor, Cap'n Jim?"

Mr. Eller pointed up the row. "From here to yonder, I reckon. We brought a handful. About four barns of sandlugs."

"Just a handful, eh?" The manager winked at Joedel, scribbling in a little notebook. "I wish I had a little handful cured up like that."

"Well, we got a lot of mouths to feed yonder at Ellers Bend."

Clint said, "And some of them mighty hungry."

Booster laughed. "Now you spreading the gospel."

The stout manager examined his notebook, then left, banging his hook against a stanchion and shouting at the sweating Negroes who were helping unload the big trucks.

"Where's your basket at, Joedel?" Mr. Jim asked. The white collar under his seersucker suit had wilted and his black bow tie had slipped sideways.

The boy caressed the carefully arranged hanks as if they were alive. The leaves were long and orangy, catching the sunshine from the skylight like a heap of broom sedge.

The ten sticks had weighed out sixty pounds even. Joedel had figured, at ten cents a pound, he would clear over five dollars after the warehouse charges and auction fee were subtracted. More than enough to buy the catcher's mitt. There would be enough left over for presents for his mother and Sissie.

Mr. Jim smiled. "I declare, it looks right pretty." Teasing, he said the basket wouldn't disgrace them—in fact, he wished now he hadn't given it away in such a big hurry.

"It does all right, that baccer," Shad agreed. "Now it do."

"You reckon it'll pass, Mr. Jim?"

Joedel watched the little Cap'n as he picked up a bundle roughly and sniffed at it. He patted the hank back in place and spit snuff juice on the floor.

"It ought to pass." He did not look at the boy squatting beside the basket.

"You reckon I ought to mark *damaged* on the ticket?" That way the ordeal would be over, all the worry about whether the buyers would detect the sweet odor of corruption on the disguised tobacco. Joedel thought, If he gives the word,

I'll mark it *damaged* and settle for two cents a pound. That way, no one can blame me for anything.

The old man pretended he had not heard, turning away.

Clint Shaw said, "Crap! Let them find it out. It's what they're paid for."

"Let me sample it," Shad said. The Negro leaned way over and smelled the top layer. Straightening up, he smiled broadly. "I know what I'm looking for," he said, "and I can't hardly make it out myself. How them men gonna tell and they in a big rush this opening day?"

Clint interposed, "Well, if they do find it, by God we'll have to take it home and make hen nests out of it. I swear it won't make the warehouse charges." And frowning, he added, "I'd feel better if it was in another row, not so close to our good tobacco."

Then they went back to the wagon and continued unloading.

There was a line of dollies waiting in front of the huge scales and Joedel and Booster had to wait. Joedel sat on the barrow and listened to the scraps of talk around him.

The farmers had been isolated during the cold winter. Except for near neighbors, they had not seen each other since last year's tobacco sales. Now was the time for talking, and they spoke as if the talk had been bottled up in them through many long nights. They conversed in small groups, standing in line or sitting on barrows and stacks of latticed crates after their tobacco was weighed and dropped in the designated place in rows as long as a football field.

"You hear about the trouble over at Hobson Sanderlin's? Well, he cut off his niggers' furnish at Sam Eller's store. Told them they couldn't get any more fatback or coffee. Would have to make out on dried peas and collards."

"They quit on him?"

"Something like it."

"Good riddance. I'd say he was lucky to get shed of

them. He got stuck with some uppity niggers that expected to live pretty high off the hog. Now the crop's all his'n."

"He got shut of them all right. Went over to his tenant house one morning and they'd cleared out, lock, stock, and barrel."

"Hadn't give him notice?"

"No, but they'd burned down both his tobacco barns."

"Well, I'll be confound. I never heard tell of such a thing. Niggers is gittin beside theirselves. They ain't the only ones hurting in this depression."

Joedel heard a sickly-looking man talking on the tenth row. "Yeah, we went over there intending to steal some of them potatoes, but we came back with our tails betwixt our logs. They'd sprayed them with kerosene or maybe some kind of poison. A little mountain of Irish potatoes, all poisoned against us. And us with younguns crying with their bellies poking out."

"You'd think it was Hoover times. Lord have mercy, all my little chaps. . . ."

"And I hear tell they're killing pigs out yonder sommers. Shootin' 'em in ditches and covering 'em up to rot. And I ain't seen a piece of bacon all winter."

"They say in Californy, the fruit just rots and falls off the trees, nothing but flies to eat it. They can't get enough to pay for picking it, yet what little gits here is so high it's out of my pocketbook's reach."

"Ain't that a curiosity for you? Folks like us with our bellies griping and they let fruit and pork rot by the tons."

"Tobacco's a pure hellish crop to raise. No other like it. Sometimes I wish I was a coal miner."

"It's the Lord's truth. You got to break your damn back to raise it, then bring it to market and American or Reynolds steals it for ten cent a pound, or some infernal pinhooker. Worse than highway robbery ever dared to be."

"You can't raise it for that, can't begin to and come out ahead."

"If you kept books and give yourself ten cent a hour, you'd be losing money, like pouring it down a crawdad hole. Am I right?"

"You can't do it. A man can't afford to count his own time. If he did, he'd despair."

Clint interrupted. "Sometimes I think it's not a crop at all. It ain't like cotton. It ain't like beans or corn or peanuts. If you can't sell them, you can bring 'em home and eat 'em or somebody can use 'em. Sometimes I think tobacco's a weed, a damn weed with a curse on it, and in the end all our sweat and labor goes up in smoke or nasty spit."

"Now you talking. Sometimes I think it's a pure sin. Maybe that gummy plant ain't nothing but a judgment sent on us, exacting pain and toil. It's a heap worse than the plagues of Egypt in the Good Book."

"Like our preacher said, cigarettes are coffin nails, and all us that raise tobacco are ungodly and compounding the sins of the world."

There was a silence, then one farmer said, "He'd better not say that around me. He'd better not, not while I've got mouths to feed and furnish to stand for at the grocery."

"I'd tell him off, too, Tully. I'd ask him where the hell he thought all the money in his dang collection plate come from. Maybe mustard patches?"

The men sitting on the dollies nodded in agreement.

Joedel listened to the rawboned farmers talking. And under all the complaints, he detected the note of pride that came when men pit themselves against a worthy adversary. He sensed that they would have it no other way, were secretly proud that their crop was the most painful and exacting to raise and took extraordinary skill before it could be displayed for neighbors to see on the auction floor. An extra fillip was added by the knowledge that their sweat and pain ultimately went up in smoke, drifting into the sky.

For Joedel, too, knew the pleasure that can be extracted from pain and toil. In the mornings hauling the tobacco from the curing barns, on Mr. Jim's truck, the wind hurt his eyes, watering them, yet he would not turn his head or close his aching eyes. Or bending over the roaring open furnace with a pine log, sometimes he stooped longer than need be, taking the full force of the heat in his face. At night after breaking suckers, he took pride in his gummy arms and salt-laden shirt, grinding the gritty soap harsher than need be into his weary flesh. Like the tobacco growers around him, he felt only pity for truck farmers who did not know what it was to raise and display golden baskets of tobacco on the auction floor. They weren't even rightly farmers, but more like gardeners.

Later, Joedel and Booster were waiting with loaded barrows at the long line before the scales. To his left Joedel saw a family of Indian farmers unloading their tobacco from a battered pickup. He watched shyly as they pulled back string quilts that were the same pattern as his mother's, observing that their tobacco was trashy and thin, almost worthless. The three Indian men wore straw hats and khaki clothing; they were talking quietly among themselves and their dark-skinned wives. Their mahogany faces seemed expressionless, and they never spoke to the whites or Negroes working around them.

In front of him, the boy saw a white farmer nudge the man beside his dolly. "Indians," he said, nodding.

"Yeah, you know what kind of Indians," the man answered with a knowing grin.

"Well, they claim to be descendants of Pocahontas or some such."

"Pokey what?"

"Pocahontas."

"You mean pokey-nigger, don't you?" Both men broke into peals of laughter. "You meant to say pokey-nigger, didn't you?" the man repeated, slapping his thigh and laughing loudly.

Joedel could hardly contain his anger and unconsciously he balled his fists up. He was on the verge of speaking when he felt Booster's hand on his arm.

For a moment Joedel looked into the dark boy's eyes, then sighed, turning away.

Booster whispered, "Don't let what them peckerwoods say bother you, Joedel. Pay no mind to such po' white trash."

The boy did not reply. Instead, he grabbed the dolly handles and rolled his heavy load recklessly toward the scales.

When their wagon was finally unloaded, Joedel drove the team outside and tied up to a hitching post in the shade of a large elm. He carefully folded Maddie's quilts around the beveled sticks and set their lunch behind the broken bale of hay.

For a moment he waited in the shade, letting his tired arms and legs rest. There were dozens of mules and wagons around him, many of the mules waiting patiently in the blazing sun. Negro children were playing under the wagons, fly-ridden babies lying on ragged quilts or sheets made of tow sacks.

In the vacant lot between the New Deal Warehouse and Cox's Mule Stables, two men were already cutting weeds, preparing for the night's free movie. Watching them swinging their lively blades, the boy felt a momentary sadness at having to miss the show. He recalled the time they had gone to the moving pictures when they had carried a load of tobacco all the way to Brownsville, the county seat of Waccamaw County.

Mr. Jim had treated them to the tent show, which was pitched in a weedy lot close to the warehouse. Joedel had sat on the hard chair by his father, alive to the excitement. There were two blackface comedians with large white lips and baggy trousers and funny long shoes, and they made the crowd roar with their capers and monkeyshines. The blacker one said he wanted them to know he wasn't his natural color: "I've been sick." Everyone laughed at that and there were more funny stunts and jokes. Finally, the fat one reached over to tie his monstrous shoe and the skinny one hit him with a wooden paddle. The noise echoed throughout the tent and Joedel wondered if it really hurt.

Then the two comedians sold boxes of candy with prizes

in them, and the fat comic held up a pretty girl's prize for everyone to see. It was a pair of pink bloomers, but he pretended it was a bathing cap. Pointing to the two leg holes, he said they were to put your ears through.

"I'll swanee, listen at his foolery now."

"He's a natural-born cutup."

After that there was a movie short in which a barbershop quartet sang "Wedding Bells Are Breaking Up That Old Gang of Mine." Then the feature film, a Ken Maynard Western. Afterward, the farmers got up stiffly, grinning shyly at each other, walking slowly back to their wagons or trucks or bedding down in the noisy warehouse.

In a moment Joedel went back inside the stifling warehouse. He needed to cap off the top of his pile so that the brightest hanks would show up. Then there would be some time for loafing before dinner and the afternoon sale. He thought of looking around for his friend Shag Squires. He wanted to show him his basket of tobacco and casually mention the baseball mitt he would soon possess.

As it happened, Joedel encountered Trudy before he started looking for Shag Squires. She yelled, waving at him from her father's Mack truck, which was being unloaded near the green scales. She turned to talk with Mr. Baldwin, who was bossing his Negro sharecroppers as they packed the tobacco, then she walked to where Joedel waited shyly. His father and Cap'n Jim were nowhere in sight, and he was glad that Mr. Baldwin had not looked in his direction.

Joedel noted that his classmate had taken a growing spell since school let out. She was now as tall as he was, in low heels, not even counting her thick auburn hair that fell around her shoulders. Her small breasts seemed to strain against her red and white checked blouse, her firm behind filling out her blue jeans.

They talked for a moment before Joedel told her he had just started to look for Shag. Then they strolled past the blind Negro singer and down the street ramp.

Joedel felt vaguely uneasy. In pretended nonchalance, he put his hands in the pockets of his jeans, narrowed his eyes against the August glare, and watched the stream of farmers passing from one steaming warehouse to the Banner, the brick warehouse across the street. There were angry bleats from the horns of trucks and cars, slowed by the wagons drawn by mules and horses.

"You'd think it was Wilmington," he said. "All this traffic." It was all he could think to say, sensing the constraint that grew between them.

"Or Raleigh or Charleston," Trudy added.

Joedel wondered if she was making the point that she had been to more distant places than he. His mother called that being "journey-proud." He did not know how to interpret her remark. Rather than ponder over it, after waiting for an empty truck to pass and suffering the leer of the driver, he took the girl gingerly by the arm and led her across the street and into the shade of the row of maples. Under his stiff fingers, Trudy's arm was soft and sweaty. The street was so hot that the tar was melting under his tennis shoes.

Before entering the warehouse, Joedel stopped before the rusty pump. It was already primed and he picked up the tin dipper.

"You want a drink?"

Trudy's mobile lips stretched with displeasure. "You're not gonna drink from that old dipper, I hope."

"Sure. I'm not gonna touch it with my lips. Look, I'll show you." Suddenly Joedel was glad for his thirst. He would turn it to his advantage by having something to show Trudy which she didn't already know. Besides, he could always talk better if he had something to hold in his hands.

Explaining how he held the dipper, Joedel drank a few swallows. He reddened under the curious blue eyes of the girl, who watched with hands on her slim hips, her head tilted like a robin's. At least, the water tasted good and he let some spill down his chin and under his shirt. Holding the edge of the dipper a half inch below his mouth, he pressed it against his chin, sucking the cool water up.

"Go ahead. You try."

Trudy shook her head, her wide mouth stretching even further. "It wouldn't be so bad, but half these folks are snuff-dippers."

A leather-faced woman waiting to drink heard her and cackled with laughter, trembling the goiter on her neck. She took the dipper, spit out her snuff, and winked at Joedel. She began pumping, still laughing soundlessly to herself, her shapeless black dress swaying. "Lord a mercy, but some younguns is hard to suit nowadays."

His brows knitted, Joedel stepped back from the stoop-shouldered woman, feeling guilty because he did not pump for her, as he was prepared to do for the girl who was so choosey and better able to pump for herself.

And turning, he spotted his friend Shag Squires. He was driving a ramshackly one-horse wagon out of the warehouse, and Joedel was surprised to see that it was loaded with tobacco piled helter-skelter, not half covered with tow-sack sheets. But in spite of his mounting curiosity, at the moment he did not want to encounter his Ellers Bend companion. Perhaps Shag had not seen him, he thought, turning quickly toward the waiting girl.

But Shag had seen them. He pulled the bony mule over to the side of the street and jerked to a halt. Nodding his hand-me-down felt hat, he grinned down at the two on the clay sidewalk, looking owlishly at Joedel.

For the first time, Joedel felt that Shag Squires was somehow inadequate. Wordless, too, he stared back at the silent boy on the wagon, whose freckled malarial face seemed blank with surprise.

Shag's left hand held the reins, and he sat carelessly on the pile of tobacco, no doubt bruising it. Joedel wondered what kind of cussing Cap'n Jim would put on any cropper he caught sitting on *his* tobacco like that! A homemade cigarette drooped from Shag's thin lips. There was green gum coating his blue work shirt, and his wrists stuck out of grimy sleeves.

Joedel looked at Shag's snub nose and hazel eyes, feeling more than ever uneasy.

"There you are, Shag. I thought I'd missed you."

Shag pushed back the greasy felt hat from his sallow face. "You right sure you been lookin' for me hard?" The skin around his eyes crinkled and his lips pulled back from stained horse teeth in a sardonic grin. He held the reins with what appeared to be a claw, for he had lost three fingers to a dynamite cap.

Joedel wished now that he had met Shag earlier, before he encountered Trudy Baldwin.

For her part, Trudy waited by his side in the elm shade, just as if she were his girl.

There was a pause.

"Won't you introduce me to your friend, Joedel?" Shag was two years behind them at the Clayton School, having failed three grades.

For a moment, the boy was filled with an unreasoning panic. As he looked up into the face of his boon companion, Shag Squires, master hunter, trapper, and raider of trotlines and fish traps, he forgot his name! His mind went blank and he watched as Shag's thin lips drew farther back from his gums.

"Trudy, I'd like you to make the acquaintance of—of Shag Squires," he blurted, finally.

Shag touched the brim of his greasy hat with his claw, and Trudy said it was a pleasure to meet him, holding her lips in a smile. She mentioned that she'd seen him in the schoolyard at recess.

Joedel noticed that Shag's eyes played over the girl as if he were judging a horse or a cow at the county fair, and he felt a rising resentment.

"Where's your old man—where's Mr. Squires at?" He recalled that Mr. Squires could not sell his tobacco any more at the New Deal Warehouse. Last year he had been caught slipping some bricks out of a basket after it had been weighed.

"At Rex Gooden's, more than likely gettin' drunk." It

turned out that Mr. Squires had had a poor sale and turned the tag on his tobacco, loading it back on his wagon in a huff.

"They said it was too green, and Pa vowed he'd take it home and let the hogs chew it before he let them steal it." He had even offered to fight the Reynold's buyer and had finally stomped out, cursing them all a blue streak.

Shag was unembarrassed, even proud, as he told of the fracas at the Red Banner. "I don't blame Pa for gittin' his dander up."

Trudy stood on tiptoe and looked at the top layer of leaves. "It looks all right to me. It looks right pretty."

"It'll do, I reckon."

Joedel agreed, but he knew better. He could see the pale green streaks running down the central stem in the leaves. That came from running the heat up too fast before the leaves had properly dried out, something his father never let happen.

Another palpable silence fell between them. Joedel started to tell Shag about having his own basket of tobacco on the floor at the New Deal, then decided against it.

"You heard the blind nigger?" Shag inquired.

Joedel said he intended to hear him, but he and Trudy were just heading behind the warehouse to check on the team of mules.

"That so? You wouldn't be going to take a little ride out past the cemetery, now, Joedel?"

Shag's laughter was as dry and mocking as a sudden twang on a banjo. Before the embarrassed boy could reply, his friend lashed the bony mule and skillfully worked the wagon into the line of traffic. As he reached McDougald's store, he turned to shout, "Roses is red, violets is blue; sugar is sweet and I love you."

Joedel wished the sidewalk would open up and swallow him.

"Don't pay that tacky boy any mind." Trudy plucked at his arm. "Let's go see about your mules, Joedel."

But first she wanted to see his little basket of tobacco.

INSIDE THE NEW DEAL AGAIN, JOEDEL GRINNED shyly at Booster while the slender girl inspected his disguised tobacco. He did not point out that it was tainted, and she did not appear to notice.

"I declare," she said, "you'll be rich. It's a pretty little basket. And you've got it packed so nice."

Joedel felt his chest expanding as a number of stout farm wives turned to look at Trudy, smiling. He casually mentioned the catcher's mitt he intended to purchase.

When the peanut salesman, a Negro boy with a ringworm on his head, came by, Joedel blurted, "Trudy, you care for some boiled peanuts?" Out of the corner of his eye, he saw Clint looking at them.

"I don't care if I do, thank you."

He bought two sacks, paying with a quarter that he had hidden in the Prince Albert can. He handed Trudy her sack awkwardly, then opened his. Booster was gazing hungrily at the sack, but Joedel pretended not to notice, turning his back on the Negro tenants and his father's inquisitive look.

He was grateful now that Maddie had trimmed his hair and made him wear shoes and his best shirt and dungarees. As he ate the soft, salty boiled nuts, he remembered not to smack, chewing with his mouth closed. He debated about offering to buy her a cold drink but decided against it, since it was close to dinnertime. The whistle at Hester's Mill would soon blow and the noisy auction across the street would grind to a halt.

"Let's walk outside," the girl said. "I'm about to melt off my bones."

Joedel followed her down the aisle, between shallow crates of tobacco, enduring the broad grins of Doll Boney and Uncle Ander and their folks.

Behind the warehouse, Trudy exclaimed, "Goodness gracious! I never saw so many wagons and carts in my born days."

Joedel broke off a part of the baled hay and gave it to the patient mules. An unshaven man in a sweat shirt was staring at Trudy and Joedel turned away, only to see a Negro woman breast-feeding a baby.

"Look at that cute baby," the girl said. "And its mother has had her ears pierced."

Joedel averted his eyes, feeling his face redden. He was astonished to see the girl looking at the dark woman's naked breast as she fed her baby, brushing the flies away with her free hand.

The boy waited impatiently for her to turn away. Then it was understood that they would take a walk before returning to eat dinner.

"Let's go look at the river, Joedel. You want to?" Her eyes were squinched in the sun's glare. "It looks cool in the shade yonder."

He felt shy and did not answer, thinking of his classmates fishing near the bridge. When she put her arm through his, he was glad his father was not present. He could imagine what Mr. Sam Eller would say at the store when Clint took back the news of him walking with a pretty girl.

He could think of nothing to say, so he told her of the pheasants Mr. Sam raised and banded in wire cages behind the store. "I help him feed 'em lots of times."

"Just to turn aloose? Why does he do that?" Trudy's forehead was wrinkled.

"I don't know. He never hunts them himself. I guess it's just because he likes to, and the pheasants are so pretty."

"That's a silly reason."

"Well, they make good eating, too." His father had killed one last fall.

They stood on the shaded bank of the Cape Fear River. For a while the boy and girl were silent under the water oak, eating the boiled peanuts. They tossed the empty shells into the river, watching until they disappeared below the cotton gin. Joedel thought of how the shells would pass under the ferry cable at Ellers Bend, then maybe on to the Atlantic Ocean.

"Goobers," Trudy laughed. "It's a funny word. How on earth did they come to call a little old peanut a goober?"

Joedel said he didn't know, but he knew a colored boy named Goober. He was the knee-baby in Uncle Ander's family. "Goober's no funnier than pender. Some people call them penders, you know."

They walked to the cotton gin and sat under the open shelter. A breeze came up from the river, lifting the girl's reddish hair. Trudy wadded up her sack and threw it into the green fennel. Joedel saw how she wrinkled her nose when she drew back to throw, stirring the clean scent of soap. Except for the bridge of freckles on her face and arms, her skin was as pale as Jean Harlow's. For a moment he felt ashamed, thinking of his mother and Sissie working in the hot packhouse at Ellers Bend while he enjoyed himself in the shade. For a moment he compared Maddie's calloused hands to Trudy's.

"Those sure hit the spot, Joedel. I like peanuts a lot better boiled than parched."

"Me too. A hundred times better."

"Last week we boiled a whole washpot and invited all

the young people . . ." Then she glanced at his face, and her
voice trailed off. "Uh—all the kids in my Sunday school class.
And Fanny Lee's. The peanut party was her idea."

He had a clear image of her older sister, for her eyes
were each a different color, one brown and one blue. He had
seen her playing hopscotch and jackrocks on the sidewalk at
school, playing with the little girls for a lark. The high school
boys crowded around her, waiting for the school bus, and he
had heard them talking of buying Victrola records and seeing
the latest moving pictures at Queen City.

Joedel pressed the last peanut. It squirted salt water and
Trudy giggled. "Old pops," she said. She wrinkled her pert nose
and looked off toward the crowded warehouse. Her mouth was
pulled down, as if the thought of returning was unpleasant.

"I just hate to go back to that warehouse, Joedel," she
said seriously. "I wish I never had to go back in there, ever."

"Why?" he asked, surprised.

"Daddy wants me to sit on that pile of his best grade. He
wants me to pretend like it's mine so the buyers will up the
price. I could skin Daddy alive for that silly stunt."

Joedel was puzzled; he could not understand her unex-
pected vehemence. He merely looked at her without saying
anything.

"It's for little girls, that sort of first-grader thing." Then
she turned abruptly as if angry with the chastened boy. "Don't
you notice anything different about me?" She sat up straight so
that her firm breasts pushed against her taut checked blouse.

Joedel looked, then reddened, his face growing hot. He
swallowed. For the first time he felt his flesh stir for a girl, and
he turned over and stretched out to cover his embarrassment,
propping his chin on one hand.

"I'm growing up," Trudy asserted, "in spite of what
Daddy thinks." She bent over close and nearly whispered,
"Why, last year a buyer pinched my—my tail! A dirty old pin-
hooker." She made a face, then broke into sudden laughter at

Joedel's solemn look, pushing her hair back. "Don't you see why I'm mad at Daddy? It's just not fair."

Joedel nodded, not smiling. He saw the delicate beads of sweat forming above her upper lip.

"Do you ever smoke, Trudy?" he asked.

"No, silly. It'll stunt your growth." She broke off a stem of a bitterweed and put it in her mouth.

Joedel noticed that she wore a light touch of lipstick, probably Fanny Lee's.

"Why did you ask that?"

He shook his head. He was thinking of his dream that maybe some day the woman he was destined to marry would smoke a cigarette made from tobacco he'd helped to raise. Soon Trudy would be old enough to smoke. She was a year older than Joedel. She had missed a year of school because of a mastoid operation that had left a deep dent behind her ear, which is why she always wore her hair longer than her sister's. She would never dip snuff, Joedel thought. That was for old women like his Grandma Oxendine and the Indian women at Pembroke.

"I never intend to smoke, not even when I'm grown up," Trudy said.

"Why?"

She stretched her lips. "I don't know why. I just think of those ugly worms and all."

"Hornyheads and budworms, too," Joedel said. "And the Paris green that's sprayed——"

"I declare, it seems enough—why, to kill the very old boogerman."

"That's why I won't smoke, too. I can't get the worms and poison out of my mind. Sometimes I dream about them."

There was a pause and the two looked at each other.

"But it doesn't scare off the others. Fanny Lee already smokes, sneaking around behind Mama's back."

Joedel agreed and said that his father chewed all the

time. He even confessed that his mother dipped snuff, but not often. "She says it helps when her teeth ache." Then he added, "I guess we must be different, Trudy."

The girl looked at him intently. "Yes, you must not be much like your parents, to feel that way."

The boy did not deny it and there was another pause, the girl waving away a persistent bee.

"It smells your perfume," Joedel said, and they both laughed.

The ache did not go away from his groin, and unconsciously Joedel bit a seed wart on his knuckle. Far down the tracks he could hear the noon freight train approaching. He thought of the pennies he and Sissie had put on the tracks once for the train to flatten.

Suddenly Trudy's blue eyes widened. "Why, Joedel, you're bleeding."

A trickle of blood was running down from the bitten wart.

It did not help his discomfiture when the girl pulled out a white hankerchief and dabbed at his hand. He noticed how her light skin made his arm seem darker.

"You been playing with toadfrogs?" Trudy said he should go see Mr. Hutch Hutchinson, who clerked at old man McDougald's store. "He can take off warts about as quick as a wink. He did Sister's. All he does is rub them with both of his hands, mumbling some voodoo stuff to himself. Then pretty soon you wake up one morning and they are gone, disappeared. It beats all."

Joedel was relieved when she took her hand away and unreasonably joyous for the topic of warts. Finally, he found some cobweb to put on his bitten finger and the trickle of blood dried up.

"Well," he said, "it's stopped bleeding."

Trudy took his hand to examine it. "It never bled much anyway. Why, I'll bet I've bled way more than you."

"I guess you have," the boy replied. He was thinking of her operation, the deep dent behind her delicate ear.

"Oh, you nasty thing!" Trudy said, blushing. "I wasn't studying that." She let his hand drop, slapping at him playfully. "You ought to wash your mouth out with yellow soap." She looked at him, teasing. "After that fresh remark, I guess it's time for us to go." She stood up, pulling at his arm. "Daddy'll be cross as two sticks."

Joedel did not understand. He let her pull him to his feet, slipping his hand into his pocket again, rubbing his knife. They watched the long train pass, feeling the earth tremble under their feet. Then they started back, walking slowly.

Trudy held his arm. "There's still time to hear the blind man sing."

As soon as they approached the warehouse, its din and stir, Mr. Baldwin saw them. He was a stocky man dressed in sweaty khaki, thick red hair curling where his shirt was unbuttoned, his chunky face splotched with pale freckles. His skull was bald on top, and what hair he had left was thin and red.

Suddenly at the top of the back ramp, he was looming above them, hairy hands on his hips.

"Trudy! I've been looking all over for you!" Her father glared down at them.

Joedel stopped uneasy.

"Where you been nohow?"

For a moment he wondered if she would stammer or falter.

"Where you been, I say?"

But Trudy was not at all disconcerted. She simply smiled and spoke to Mr. Baldwin in a quiet voice that betrayed no intimacy between them. "Daddy, this is my friend, Joedel."

The boy marveled at the ease with which she walked up the cluttered ramp ahead of him, one hand brushing a wisp of hair away from her forehead. He was careful not to look at her bottom.

As he lagged behind, in the wake of her clean scent, he felt his skin prickle under the slitted eyes of her hostile father. Joedel walked blindly, stepping on the edge of a pile of horse manure. She had not mentioned his last name, and he could not bring himself to say it now. Instead, he scraped his worn tennis shoe awkwardly, looking off across the straight rows of crated tobacco, watching the sun through the skylights catch the motes dancing in the stifling air. He did not see Clint or Cap'n Jim anywhere.

Trudy and her father were talking now between themselves heatedly, and Mr. Baldwin's face grew even redder.

"Don't you dare sass me, little miss."

"Daddy, I'd purely be ashamed. I've never been so embarrassed in . . ."

Her voice rose so that a farmer wheeling an empty dolly turned to stare.

"You heard me now. You put your little butt in that cab and stay there till we eat. You don't, this is the last time I ever bring you to market."

"I declare to goodness, I already told you we never——"

But he was already taking her arm and propelling her toward the black truck with high sidings.

Then he turned on the stunned boy, his hazel eyes cold as flint. "Whose boy are you, nohow?"

For a long moment Joedel could not speak, his mouth was so dry. A car horn blew angrily, a man lashing a team of gray horses away from the scales. Then he blurted his name out, overcome with embarrassment, the crestfallen girl looking away. It was obvious that the name meant nothing to Mr. Baldwin.

Then proudly, "We farm for Mr. Jim Eller."

"It don't matter a good damn." He spit a stream of tobacco juice toward the boy's rooted tennis shoes. His angry eyes studied Joedel's mane of dark hair, his coppery face. Then his thin lips warped into a smile.

"You a nigger, boy?" he asked.

"Daddy!" Trudy's voice was shrill with indignation.

"I say, are you a conk-haired nigger?"

Joedel's head jerked back as if he had been slapped. He felt his breath expel and the muscles around his chest tighten painfully.

"Joedel's part Indian," Trudy was explaining. "He's part Croatan."

But he did not hear the rest. Suddenly, of their own volition, his feet were turning, his stiff legs propelling him down the littered ramp toward the promise of fresh air.

"I don't care a damn what you are. I'll thank you to stay away from my daughter, boy." Mr. Baldwin bellowed after him. "You don't, then I know how to take care of such trash as you."

Joedel could hear Trudy crying now above the noises of the warehouse, but curiously he did not care. There was a sickening numbness in his legs, a strange feeling in his loins. Although he did not formulate it into thoughts, all he wished at the moment was to get out of the warehouse. If he did not, he thought that he would vomit.

He crawled under the two-horse wagon, wishing it were a cave, and let his hot face rest on the cool grass, ignoring the laughter of the Negro children playing around him.

XIV

AT NOON, WHEN THEY WENT TO THE WAGON TO eat, their dinner had been stolen. Joedel's blue jumper was there by the broken bale of hay and Grapette bottle, but the bowl in the paper sack was gone.

"That's a pretty come-off," Mr. Eller said.

"I'll be a son-of-a-bitch," Clint swore.

Joedel read the sudden fury in his father's face. He had seen a white man hanging around the wagon, noting his sharp, bearded face and ragged sweat shirt, but now he made no mention of it. Nor did he speak of the encounter with Trudy's father.

Shadrach said, "You all welcome to share with us, Mistuh Clint. We got more'n a gracious plenty."

Booster smiled. "Mama fixed us a bait of black-eyed peas and rice."

Joedel would have liked to share the hoppin john, but he saw his father shake his head curtly, lines of irritation etched above his nose.

"No thank you, Booster," Joedel replied.

Clint Shaw said, "I reckon we'll grab us a bite yonder at that café."

In Joedel's remembrance his father had never set foot in the warehouse café, or any restaurant.

Clint angrily ripped open the bale of hay and dropped it in front of the mules. The two mules began eating, switching the flies away with their tails.

Mr. Eller said he was heading toward the hotel, and they walked with him, leaving the Negroes eating in the shade of the elm. This was Mr. Jim's one extravagance, to eat the family-style dinner served at the old three-story hotel, swapping yarns with the buyers and other tobacco men. Under one arm he carried a blunted plow sweep that he intended to leave at the blacksmith shop.

They parted in front of the New Deal Warehouse. Joedel watched Mr. Jim's short legs as he picked his way up the crowded sidewalk, walking toward the water tower and hotel. Sweat stained the back of his rumpled seersucker coat.

They were inside Lamb's Café. It was the first time Joedel had ever ordered a meal in his life, and he felt as awkward as if someone had sent him to make a phone call in an emergency. Joedel studied his father secretly. He was behaving as if eating in a café were an everyday occasion with him. The boy held the menu up stiffly, imitating his father, rigid with a sense of decorum.

As he looked at the menu, Clint's forehead was creased. The café served only two meals, barbequed pork and Brunswick stew.

"How's your barbeque?" Clint asked the large-bosomed waitress, whom he had known in his cotton-mill days before his marriage. He could hardly be heard above the bustle and gabble of voices. The café was crowded with sweaty farmers standing between the crowded tables. They were anxious to eat before the sale in the New Deal commenced, scraping their brogans impatiently as they waited for empty seats.

"It's good," Sarah Thelma said, smiling pertly. "Would

you believe I cooked it myself?" She laughed a throaty laugh. Joedel noted the way she stood close to his father, rubbing her hip against his elbow. He compared her thick waist with Trudy's trim figure. There were faint hairs on her upper lip, beaded with sweat.

Clint grinned. "In that case gimme the Brunswick stew. Is there any squirrel in it?"

The plump waitress grimaced. "You know what you can do with your squirrel. Damn long-tailed rats." All the time she was writing in her little pad.

"What about you, sonny?"

The dark-haired waitress's lively eyes were on him, as though she had guessed he'd never ordered a meal before. Suddenly Joedel's throat went dry as if he were on the stage alone at Clayton High. He swallowed and gripped the menu, staring at it grimly.

"I didn't hear you."

Finally he blurted out that he wanted a hamburger with a grape Nehi.

"I believe your boy's bashful, Clint," Sarah Thelma teased. She winked. "Not like his daddy. I mean, not like his daddy *use* to be in the old days."

She asked Clint if he still had his guitar. He said he'd sold it. He did not mention that he'd traded it for an Oliver plow.

"I'll take that now."

"What? Oh." Joedel sheepishly handed her the menu.

"Where's Clarence these days?" Clint asked.

"Clarence? Who's he?" The waitress made a face. "I wouldn't be knowing. Last I heard he was down there in Florida somewheres."

Clint inquired about her daughter.

"He took Shirley with him." Flashing a smile, she added, "That leaves me footloose and fancy free, you might say."

"You left that cotton mill for good?"

"I sure God have. It's about time I got out of that god-

forsaken cotton-mill dump." Her husky voice took on a bitter
edge and Joedel saw the hard lines that ran down from her nose
to the wide full mouth, her black frizzled hair that hung to her
shoulders. Her mouth was as hard as a circus lady's.

"I can't say as I miss the mill much myself," Clint said.

"It's pure hell and I'm glad it's shut down." Then she
asked, "Who you farming for nowadays?"

"I'll soon be farming for myself." Clint said he was tending a place for old man Jim Eller this season. He did not use the
word *sharecropper.*

When Sarah Thelma set the food before them, father and
son began to eat rapidly. Joedel's confidence returned and he
wished Shag Squires would pass by on the sidewalk and see
him eating in the warehouse café. No doubt his eyes would bug
out.

In spite of the noon rush, the waitress did not leave their
table. Standing by Clint, she primped her hair, then her hand
dropped lightly on the dark hair at Clint's neck.

Joedel sat silently while his father bragged to the
woman about the down payment he would soon make on the
piece of land. He had finished. He pretended to be full, while
his father smiled expansively under the approval of his acquaintance from the old cotton-mill days. The angry lines had
gone from around his mouth.

"How much you got on the floor today?"

"Five piles. No, six, counting a little dab that belongs to
Joedel." But his father didn't stop there. He said they were the
prettiest baskets offered for sale by any of Cap'n Jim's tenants,
and the old man had had to reserve half a row. "I cured it all
up, the entire barn, as bright as gold. Mr. Jim said as much
himself. Said he'd never seen a barn of primers color up as
pretty."

"Why, I'll bet you have something to celebrate after that
auction."

Clint pushed the empty plate back. He had sopped it
clean with half a bakery roll.

Joedel looked away, thinking, He never said how light

the five piles are, hail hurt, not to mention my pile tainted with rot.

"What row you all on?"

"Row thirteen, the far end." Mr. Jim always demanded a row directly under the skylights, where the sun lit up the pressed leaves, bringing out their true color.

Sarah Thelma said she'd get off at 2:30 and come see how the sale went for them. "Ha, I might want to borrow some money off of you rich folks."

The stout man behind the counter called, "Sarah Thelma, Number 3."

"All right," she cried, irritably. "Hold your horses."

When she brought the bill, pushing her way through the crowded tables and impatient farmers, she placed a piece of chess pie and a clean fork before Clint.

"I never ordered no pie."

"I'd've swore you said chess pie. All this infernal racket."

Then she winked, flipping over the bill to show he had not been charged. "Old friends should stick together. You know what I mean?"

The boy looked at the pie hungrily. Running behind the wagon on the highway, he had worked up an appetite.

"What about him? Be a sport and buy the boy a piece of pie, Clint."

Clint's forehead was furrowed, and Joedel looked at him, wooden-faced. "I ain't hungry now, Papa." He said he'd already eaten some peanuts.

"Peanuts," the waitress said. "Hell, be a spender. You ain't forgot it's opening day? Time to celebrate."

Joedel sensed what an effort it cost his father to shake his head, scowling. With his fork, he crushed the pie in two, handing the boy the wedge end. He stood up abruptly. "We can eat this on our way out."

When he paid the bill at the door, he nodded at the smiling waitress, who stuck out the pink tip of her tongue, tilting her head.

"If I get off in time, I'll sure come see you all's sale."

"You do that thing," Clint said over his shoulder. "And much obliged for the pie."

"Don't ever say I never give you anything." She laughed huskily. "Right?"

Joedel looked at her full painted lips and fleshy hips, thinking of his mother's bulging stomach. He could not interpret the bright flecks in Sarah Thelma's expressive eyes, but all the same he felt uneasy.

As he followed Clint's long steps up the front ramp, he surreptitiously threw the piece of pie into a clump of weeds. In the stifling warehouse his father walked tall and straight, as if he already owned the piece of land.

XV

THAT AFTERNOON THE SET OF BUYERS WAS LATE
in arriving at the New Deal Warehouse. Joedel pretended to
busy himself with rearranging the rounded top layer of his pile
of tobacco, but actually he was keeping a sharp lookout for Mr.
Baldwin. Through a rear window he had seen Trudy sitting dis-
consolately in the black truck, and once he turned his head to
avoid her father's hostile eyes.

When the buyers and the auctioneer finally arrived,
mopping their faces as they straggled up the ramp past the
blind Negro singer, Joedel did not feel the excitement he had
expected. He squatted by his basket, watching as the eager
farmers rushed toward the first row, a small cluster of wives
and children following. As he watched, the moon-faced warehouse owner gestured, the buyers fell into two ragged lines, jos-
tling one another. There was a momentary hush, then the auctioneer's rapid spiel commenced and the two rows of men
inched forward: "Nine-nine-nine-ten-lil-dolla." The sale had
begun.

Joedel waited by his shallow basket over an hour, sweat

running down his ribs like tickling ants. Once he noticed the large-breasted waitress at the end of their row. She was shading her eyes and looking in his direction.

But when the buyers neared his row, he could no longer keep still. Finally, he stood up and joined his father and Mr. Eller, who were following the buyers closely, occasionally picking up the sales tickets to glance at the prices.

As the buyers neared his basket Joedel felt his heart constrict, his scalp tingle. He forgot all about his tired legs and the encounter with Mr. Baldwin. He could not turn his eyes away from the bored faces of the buyers.

Now Mr. Eller stepped in close, his bow tie askew. He was whispering to Mr. Barefoot, the warehouse owner, and pointing to Joedel. They were at his small basket of primers, and he felt his breath grow short.

Mr. Barefoot was tearing at the heap of tobacco, destroying the pattern that the boy had carefully built, with the brightest leaves on top. He seemed to pounce on the hapless hanks, beating two bundles against each other ferociously, raising motes of dust in the air. Then he plunged his jowly face into the spread leaves as if he'd suddenly decided to bite them with his strong teeth.

Joedel let the air expel from his lungs.

"All right," Mr. Barefoot cried. "Help Cap'n Eller out here, fellas. This weed belongs to his grandson yonder. Help the boy out, I say. Don't steal his fine tobacco, you sorry rascals." He tossed the bright hanks back on the basket as the buyers stooped to their work, faces glistening."

Before Joedel knew it, the auctioneer had settled on ten cents and his tobacco had been sold. His ears were ringing and Booster was pounding him on the back. As the bunched line of buyers passed, he leaped across a heaped crate and snatched up his ticket. The sales marker had scrawled "10¢" on the slip.

"There you are," Booster exclaimed. "What'd I tell you now? Joedel, you're some kind of rich."

The boy was so elated over his triumph that he was only

vaguely aware that something was wrong a little way up the row. The steady spiel of the auctioneer had faltered, stopped. There was a moment's hush, a scuffle of feet on the sandy floor, then the manager was calling the buyers back. The auctioneer began again, but this time his voice was pitched lower as the buyers exchanged the questionable hanks, sniffing them gingerly. They let them drop, as if they had lost interest.

When Joedel turned to his father, Clint Shaw's face was dark as a thundercloud. His fist knotted around the sales ticket, Mr. Eller frowning behind him. Shadrach and Booster looked puzzled.

Smiling, Joedel held his sales slip out. "Papa, I got ten——"

Suddenly Clint slapped him hard across the mouth. His head jerked sideways and tears sprang into his eyes. Too late, he threw up an arm to ward off the blow.

"You shouldn't of did that, Mistuh Clint," Shadrach said.

Mr. Eller was tugging at his father's elbow. In the excitement, snuff juice dribbled from a corner of his mouth. "Hold on now, Clinton."

"What's wrong, Papa?" The boy tried to hide the desolation in his heart.

Clint Shaw scowled darkly. "I told you to keep that damn rotten mess away from my good tobacco. If I told you once I told you a thousand times."

"Me and Mama kept——"

"You and Mama nothing."

"Wait, Clinton," Mr. Eller interposed. He could barely be heard above the auctioneer's chant.

"Now you got some mixed in and they just bought my A grade for four cents a pound. The bastards bid it off as damaged."

"We've not got it mixed." Joedel was stubborn, hurt by the injustice. He wiped his eyes with his sleeve.

"Old Joedel," Shad said, smiling. "I know most Joedel be's careful."

"Careful," Clint spat contemptuously. He threw the boy one of the damaged bundles. "Maybe you claim that hank's not tainted."

Joedel could smell the faint sweet scent of rot before the leaves touched his nose. When he looked up, all of their eyes were on him. A small knot of farmers had gathered, men waiting to sell on the fourteenth row, when the set of buyers would turn back at the end of the long warehouse.

"Well? What do you say now?" his father demanded.

Joedel looked away, blinking back the tears. The straggly line of buyers had almost reached the end of the row, with the overalled farmers crowding in behind them grabbing up their sales slips. When he looked down at the offending hank of limp leaves, his eyes narrowed.

"What do you say, boy?"

"It's damaged all right."

"Huh," Clint snorted, looking at Mr. Eller. "I told you as much, Cap'n Jim. This is partly your own fault. You meant well, but you shouldn't've give my boy any rotten tobacco."

"It's rotten, but this ain't none of my tobacco, Papa. Anybody can see it don't belong to my pile." Joedel held the tied end out for all of them to examine. "Whoever tied this is left-handed. You know Mama and me both tie right-handed."

It was true. Maddie had tied every hank, with Joedel making the bundles for her while she folded the limp tie leaves.

Booster and Shad both broke into wide grins, nudging each other.

Booster blurted, "It's the Lord's truth, that's a left-handed tie."

Clint Shaw snatched the bundle back, examining it closely. Almost reluctantly he admitted that Joedel was right, Maddie hadn't tied that hank. Then he scooped the other rotten hanks off the top of the pile, comparing them. None of them matched his tobacco, which was short-leafed from the hail damage.

Mr. Eller nodded and spoke one word. "Planted?"

Shad smiled at Joedel, tapping his kinky skull with a dark finger.

"By God," Clint said. "By God, I smelled a rat all the time." He snatched up the sales slip again and stared at it, frowning.

Mr. Eller spit snuff juice on the floor. "I'll wager it was some pinhooker bought it."

"Them there hanks was planted, shore," Shad said. "Some low-lived scannel about to steal your best tobacco, Mistuh Clint."

"Nothing but." Clint scowled at the crumpled paper and read off the buyer's name. "Stegall." He repeated the name. "By damn, somebody's gonna pay for this little stunt, I mean to tell you."

"Hold on, now," Mr. Eller cautioned.

"Whoo-ee," Booster said to Joedel, "now we're gonna see some action."

The farmers, who had gathered in close, muttered among themselves. They looked at the boy with approval in their eyes.

It did not occur to Clint Shaw to apologize for striking his son. Wheeling, he strode up the aisle between the rows of baskets, closely followed by the grim-faced farmers.

The buyers had stopped at the end of the disordered row, the sweaty auctioneer breaking off his high-pitched chant. The stout warehouse owner had yelled for the water boy, and they were pushing chunks of ice aside and drinking from the tin dipper. The gaudy shirts of the buyers were glued to their skins with sweat and, drinking, they let the icy water dribble down their necks. They drank silently, mopping at their faces and necks with towels and handkerchiefs before lifting the dipper from the galvanized pail.

"Your name Stegall?"

The rangy speculator let the dipper fall back into the beaded bucket. Joedel watched his green eyes narrowing as if he were aiming a rifle, one hand brushing at his red mustache.

It was the tall stranger whose offer they had declined before unloading the wagon.

"I'm Stegall," he said. "Yeah."

Without a word, Clint shoved the three rotten hanks at the reddening speculator.

"What's all this about?"

The buyers stopped drinking and their faces became less bored.

"Shaw," the warehouse owner cried, "what's come over you?"

"Nothing, Mr. Barefoot. Except this son-of-a-bitch here just tried to steal a basket of my tobacco, my best grade."

"You better watch your mouth," the speculator said, "whoever in hell you are."

Mr. Eller started to explain to the warehouse owner, but Clint interrupted. "You heard me, mister. I just called you a low-down thievin' son-of-a-bitch. I'll thank you to step out back now." He jerked his thumb toward the nearby exit.

There was a hurried examination of the damaged hanks and Mr. Eller showed a sample of good tobacco from Clint's basket. The squirrel-faced auctioneer and the floor manager compared the bright leaves. Mr. Eller pointed out the difference in the ties, and the two men nodded, agreeing.

A half circle of overalled farmers had formed around the buyers, their sunburned faces as somber as if they were at a funeral.

"By granny," one said, "you work like a slave to make it, and they try to steal it off of you at the market. Hard times or no."

"It's the God's truth. Don't back down none, Shaw."

There was a moment of silence, and Joedel felt a tightening in his chest. He watched as the buyers turned their drawn smiles toward the lanky pinhooker wearing the fancy hat.

"They got it all wrong, Mr. Barefoot," Stegall whined. "I've not planted any rotten tobacco and I'm not about to." There was a little space cleared around him, the other speculators edging back to the wall, away from the grim-faced farmers.

The warehouse owner looked at him disgustedly. He told Mr. Eller there had obviously been a mix-up, but he was sure they could clear it up to everybody's satisfaction. "Damn it to hell, nobody's gonna get swindled in my warehouse. Not if I know it, they ain't." He looked at the serious faces of the farmers around him and the Negro sharecroppers who had eased back to the fringes of the tense crowd.

"You mighty right about that," Clint said. Leaning toward the speculator, he lowered his voice. "I reckon you heard what I called you, Mister. Now you'll step out back or I'll whip your butt right here before God and all those folks."

The buyers stirred uneasily, watching the two men facing each other.

"I came here to buy tobacco," Stegall said, "not fight." His bottle-green eyes glanced at the regular buyers, whose faces were fixed in sneers or looks of disbelief.

"By damn, we'll just see about that!"

A shoe hit the empty water pail and it clanged. As if it were a signal, the two men sprang at each other.

"Push 'em out back!" Mr. Barefoot cried. "Push 'em on out of my warehouse now."

As Joedel stumbled down the ramp, he picked up a broken tobacco stick. He could hear the furious blows of the two fighting men. They were cursing and pummeling each other, with the farmers shouting encouragement to Clint. Men who never spoke to him in Ellers Bend were now on his side, venting their hatred on the dishonest speculator. It was the first time a pinhooker had been challenged in years, and this was enough to make up for their disappointment in the prices on the auction.

"By God, if Shaw don't beat him, I'm gonna whup him myself."

The boy could see nothing over the heads of the shouting spectators. Finally, when he could no longer bear the suspense, he ducked his head and bulled his way forward. Shutting his eyes, he pushed his way through the dense overalled legs.

As his son broke into the little clearing, Clint shoved Stegall away, and he slipped back. The boy saw his father brush at the stream of blood from his nose. His sleeves were rolled up, and there were flecks of blood on his shirt. His dark hair was disheveled and he was panting. Sweat trickled down the army tattoo when he raised his left arm, holding his right fist on guard.

"That's just a sample, pinhooker. I'm gonna teach you what comes of cheating us farmers."

Stegall glared at him with his bottle-green eyes. All at once his hand was blurring toward his side pocket.

Cap'n Jim said weakly, "Look out for the knife, Clinton."

The crowd of onlookers surged back. Then suddenly Joedel's stick leaped out as quick as a snake's tongue. It hit the pinhooker's wrist and the switchblade skittered into the grass. At the same second, Clint's right fist smacked into Stegall's jaw. His knees buckled like a calf that has been axed in the head, and he pitched forward on his face.

"Come on," a sharecropper near Joedel cried. "Let's kill the sorry rogue."

But the pinhooker was saved from the kicking brogans. Just as the mob of outraged farmers closed in, Mr. Barefoot shouted, "Look to Cap'n Jim!"

Mr. Eller had let out a weak cry, then slumped forward in the trampled weeds. Joedel felt a numbness seize him. He could not see the still form of Cap'n Jim. A stout buyer bent over the fallen man. He leaned down so quickly that the seat of his trousers split, exposing a stretch of white underwear.

"Send for Doctor Clay," the stout man cried. "Looks like Cap'n Eller's had a stroke."

"Stand back, folks," Mr. Barefoot shouted. "Don't crowd in. Let the man have some air now."

The boy let himself be elbowed back from his stricken friend. Before he realized it, he was separated from Clint and Shadrach, wandering on the fringe of the swelling crowd. When he looked up, he saw that Stegall had recovered. The dishonest pinhooker was running toward the river, then he dashed around the warehouse corner and disappeared.

In the confusion Joedel drifted around the edge of the milling crowd of farmers and tobacco men.

"It's old man Eller," he heard a man say. "He's had a bad stroke from seeing that fight."

"Maybe it's only the heat," a woman said. "This heat's enough a kill a body."

There were more cries to send for Doctor Clay, and finally a car roared off. This was a waste of effort, for Doctor Clay was at the New Deal Warehouse checking on his tenants' tobacco. Presently he appeared, and the old man was raised gently and put on the back of his truck. Joedel could not see above the heads of the swarming farmers, but Mr. Jim's head rested on the folded tarpaulin and he lay on the Star of Bethlehem quilt Shadrach passed up to Mr. Barefoot.

As the boy watched, the doctor climbed up on the truck body. He stood tall in the burning sunlight, his white shirt open at the neck. The watchers fell silent as he stooped, then knelt over the stricken man, examining his pulse and heartbeat.

"Now we'll know something," a farmer said.

"Yeah, he'll give us the word."

Joedel climbed on a drink crate by the warehouse, but all he could see was Mr. Jim's white head, his face turned away from the harsh sun.

Doctor Clay, kneeling over the unconscious form, spoke. "Can you hear me, Mr. Eller?"

There was no answer, only a slight breeze lifted a white lock from the still forehead.

"Well, you hold on now," the doctor was speaking directly into the old man's ear. "I'll do all I can to help you, Cap'n Jim."

"You hear that?"

"Maybe he'll be all right now—if he ain't already gone."

Then Doctor Clay was shouting. "All right now, damn it, get this truck over to my office."

As the boy watched, Shadrach sprang into the driver's seat. He ground the starter but the motor only coughed and knocked off. Then Clint Shaw appeared, his right eye already swelling. Shadrach passed him the crank and he was cranking the truck furiously while the wide-eyed Negro choked the engine.

"Twist her tail off," Doctor Clay shouted.

As the motor caught and held, a two-horse wagon pulled down the ramp.

"Get those goddamn hayburners out of the way!" the furious doctor cried.

The Indian driver lashed at the horses, and they leaped up, their front hoofs pawing the air.

In a moment the truck rattled beyond the warehouse, the doctor still kneeling beside Mr. Eller, his gray-streaked hair blown back over his bald spot.

Joedel stepped down from the cold drink box as the tense farmers began to mill around, talking excitedly. He did not see Clint, who had stayed behind to tend to the sale. Booster and Uncle Ander slumped dejectedly on the wagon under the elm tree.

"You hear what the Cap'n said when Doctor Clay yelled in his ear?"

"He didn't say nary a word."

"The hell you say."

"I ought to know. I was standing right there and his face was twisted like it was an awful stroke. I tell you, he never come to."

"No, but he smiled. I seen that much."

"That could be gas pains. I never saw any smile."

"Well, what do you think? You know so much?"

"I don't give him a Chinaman's chance. He's a goner."

"I wouldn't know about that. He's an Eller and they're tough. They say Ellers don't never die, you have to hit 'em in the head with a lighterd knot."

There was a cackle of laughter and the expressions on the faces around Joedel became less serious.

A newcomer approached. "What's all the commotion about here? I just got in town. Heard a man was killed in a knife fracas."

Joedel listened intently as the stranger was filled in on

what passed for the facts. Everyone seemed eager to rehash the story, reciting a different version, adding to and correcting the others. For the moment they forgot about the aborted auction and the tobacco they had brought to sell.

"They was about to steal a crate of his tobacco with some planted rotten hanks. Mr. Jim got wrought up about it and that's what killed him."

"He ain't dead yet."

"No, but if he dies, that'll be the cause of it, to my opinion."

"They're stealin' it all anyhow, the prices they offer."

"Yeah," the tall man said. "We ought to do something. We ought to organize and hold it off the market till they meet our prices. Then we wouldn't always be over the barrel, defenseless like."

The farmers looked at the stranger nervously. Then one said, "I'd admire to do that very thing, Mister. Only thing wrong is once you take that baccer home, you sure as hell can't eat it or wear it. My younguns need grub to eat and some rags to put on their backs."

"Now you talking, neighbor."

The auctioneer and buyers had walked back up the ramp. They glanced nervously at the crowd of murmuring farmers and their tight-lipped wives.

Mr. Barefoot grinned and spoke brightly, "All right, folks, we're sorry for this unfortunate incident. Doctor Clay told me confidentially he thought Mr. Eller would be just fine. He just fainted from the heat. Let's get back in the warehouse now. Sale's resuming. Let's go get it, boys."

"Going back in to steal a few more piles?" a man asked bitterly.

The jowly owner did not appear flustered. "No sir. I run an honest warehouse here. We're gonna make amends to Mr. Eller for that unfortunate mix-up. I'm satisfied some rotten tobacco just got mixed in with his, that's all. The whole thing's an unfortunate accident."

It was then that Joedel saw Clint. He was standing

behind the buyers, looking anxiously over the crowd. The boy began to push and shove his way up the ramp. But he was trapped in the set of buyers and pushed back toward the water pail.

He heard the floor manager say to the buyers, "By jove, Burke Stegall got his today. He got just what he deserved after all he's pulled in these here warehouses."

As the auctioneer and buyers walked up the row toward Clint's basket of disputed tobacco, Joedel pushed free. He leaped over two loaded crates, walking beside the farmers. They were smiling now as the buyers returned to the disordered basket which had caused the crisis.

"Who's the feller that crawled that pinhooker's hump?"

"Cropper name of Shaw. Feller that married an Injun squaw, the way I heard it. A Croatan from upwards Pembroke."

"Well, I don't care if he married a nigger. My hat's off to him."

"It's a solid fact. He's got the old grit," a farmer from Ellers Bend said. "He's a near neighbor of mine."

It took less than a minute to auction off the disputed pile of tobacco. It brought the unheard-of price of thirty cents a pound, bought, of course, by the warehouse owner himself. Mr. Barefoot turned to the crowd of farmers, beaming, talking jovially as he led the buyers back to start in on the new row.

Joedel saw his father smiling broadly. He was showing the ticket to incredulous farmers and smiling as though Mr. Eller had not been felled as a consequence of the basket of tobacco. The boy stared in disbelief, unable to believe that his father had forgotten so soon.

Already, the Negroes were sheeting up the sold tobacco. They were stripped to the waist, their dark muscles gleaming with sweat, like wild grapes with the dew on them. They were talking and joking among themselves, a separate world, ignoring the auctioneer's spiel, the excitement of the buyers' bidding. They manhandled the huge crates of tobacco like stevedores, seizing them arrogantly and flipping them over on to the tow-sack sheets. Scooping up the ends of the sheets, they swiftly tied the two knots and tossed the loaded sheet upon the square frame with casters, rolling it with one hugely veined arm toward the doorway, where the high-sided trucks were waiting.

As Joedel watched, a Negro worker looked at the ticket on his puny basket. Smiling, he picked the light crate up and held it aloft with one untrembling arm.

"That's Mister Armstrong for you," he said to his partner, tipping the latticed crate into the spread sheet.

It was his first sale at the auction and Joedel watched his pile of tobacco as it tumbled into the rough tow sheet. His dark eyes watched as the two Negroes heaved another loaded sheet on his, then started the jack rolling across the rough floor toward the waiting truck. Above the squeaking casters he heard the blind Negro singing in his corner.

"Wait!" he almost called out. He was reluctant to see the tobacco go.

The boy looked away and his eye caught an ad for Camel cigarettes on the wall; a blonde woman who looked like Jean Harlow, wearing jodhpurs, was smoking. He blushed, remembering his dream that maybe a beautiful woman would smoke the tobacco he had harvested and cured, maybe even the woman he would grow up to marry.

When he looked back, his sheet of tobacco was gone.

"Where you been, boy?" Clint asked gruffly. "We'll go get our check now at the window yonder." He said Mr. Barefoot had arranged to pay him, even though Mr. Eller was not there to sign the checks. "He damn well better. He don't want his warehouse to get the name of cheating farmers."

Joedel walked with his father to the ticket window. Although he did not wish to think of it now, he was wondering how much above the price of the mitt his basket of disguised tobacco had brought.

XVII

ANOTHER SMALL CROWD CONGREGATED BEFORE the cashier's window at the front of the warehouse and it was the same at the Cape Fear Bank a half block up the street. Farmers gathered around Clint on the sidewalk, clapping him on the back or shaking his swollen hand. Some who had not heard of the fight congratulated him on the thirty-cents-a-pound sale. Joedel watched his father smiling expansively. At the bank he crammed the crisp bills in his wallet, then folded the sales tickets into his overall bib.

When they walked back to the warehouse there was heartening news of Mr. Eller. Someone reported that he had come to and had sent a note to the New Deal so that Clint could get his half of the money from the auction. For the first time since his tobacco was sold, Joedel felt a surge of exhilaration.

As they walked behind the warehouse to water the mules, they encountered Kirk Wiles with the large-bosomed waitress by his side. She had changed to a flowery print dress, one she had not sweated through. As they talked to Clint two or three other men drifted from the noisy warehouse, where the sale continued. The auctioneer's spiel could barely reach them.

Kirk Wiles smiled. "We heard what you done to that sorry pinhooker. We're right proud."

The others nodded. Joedel noticed that they were the sullen men he had often seen in Mr. Sam's store, farmers who only scowled at his father or nodded curtly.

Kirk's lips were pulled back from his yellow-stained teeth. He jerked a thumb over his shoulder. "I got a little taste yonder in that garage."

Clint shook his head. "I don't reckon I need any."

"It ain't costing you a red cent."

Sarah Thelma took him by the arm. "Come on and have a little snort, Clint. Don't miss a chance like this to have a little celebration, and it free." She laughed huskily, winking at Joedel.

The boy looked at her blankly, his uneasiness spreading, for the first time aware of her heavy perfume. Then he watched in disbelief as Clint was led to the gray-weathered garage beyond the hitching posts. Behind him he heard a horse whicker.

"Papa," he said. "It's time we . . ."

No one paid any attention to him. The overalled men were laughing. One reached over and slapped the waitress on the bottom and she shrieked in mock indignation. Walking, the sallow-faced bootlegger kept a hand on Clint's shoulder.

In the cool earth-smelling garage, a crap game was going on in the back, farmers kneeling on the chocolate-colored ground.

The sharp-faced bootlegger reached in a trash barrel and, as if by magic, came up with a half-filled fruit jar, unscrewing the lid with a flourish.

"Look at that bead," he said proudly. "That's the prime bottle-in-barn, if I do say so myself."

The waitress drank first, making a face. Someone handed her a soft drink and she took a swallow hurriedly, fanning a hand in front of her mouth as if her throat were on fire.

"That's strong tanglefoot, man," she said.

Scarcely believing what he saw, Joedel watched as Clint

Shaw drank from the open jar, his Adam's apple bobbing. The raw whiskey made Clint's eyes water, and he let some spill down his chin and under his work shirt. All the time he kept his eyes from meeting Joedel's.

"Go ahead on, man," Kirk insisted. "It'll take your mind off your worries and help you, too. It'll take the pain out of that swolled-up hand."

One of the crapshooters said, "We know you're worried about old man Eller."

"That's the truth. Me and Joedel think the world of that old man. He's done a heap for us, and if—"

"Hell, we all do. Just quit your worrying now."

Clint turned away from his son and took another long pull from the fruit jar, swallowing without stopping for a breath. The dimly lit garage was filled with the smell of corn whiskey.

"Look at him. Hot damn, I reckon."

Sarah Thelma laughed. "Clint use to be a real sport. Up there at the Badger Mill he use to be one more hell-bred tiger." She turned to Joedel. "Did you know your daddy was a ring-tailed sport? He use to get out among the girls and raise pure Cain." Then she added, "Before he got married, I mean."

Clint frowned and handed the empty jar back to Kirk Wiles, who fished out another full one. "Plenty more where that'n come from."

A few minutes later, Joedel felt a numbness come over him when Clint was invited into the crap game. At first his father shook his head stubbornly, but the waitress egged him on. "Be a sport, Clint. They don't ask just anybody to play. Yesterday, you couldn't'a got in. They wouldn't of let you on account of your——" She stopped in time.

The boy thought, She was going to say on account of your Indian wife. He felt miserable when he thought of his mother and Sissie working in the hot packhouse, while they dawdled and joked and celebrated. But at least they were spared, as yet, the news of Cap'n Jim's stroke.

A minute later Clint was shaking the dice, rubbing them

under his arm, a half-dozen new bills in his fist. His eyes had a fevered look in them that was strange to his son.

"Papa." Joedel had to call twice. "Papa."

The half-dozen men waited, crouched around the dice, with the dark-haired woman leaning over his father, her left hand playing at the nape of his neck.

"What you want, boy?"

"We'd better start back now."

Clint did not look up. "You go ahead on. I'll catch up directly. You water the mules and I'll come on directly so we can do our trading."

The boy did not leave and Kirk Wiles turned to wait on a new customer, a man in striped overalls.

Joedel looked at the waitress, then at his father. "I need —I want my money now from the sale." He hated himself for asking for it in front of her.

"We'll settle up later, boy. You know we never got our full share on account of Cap'n Jim's stroke. I'll be——"

Suddenly, the waitress erupted. "For Pete's sake, Clint, give your boy his money and let him go shopping. You said yourself that basket was all his. None of it was old man Eller's."

The man with the dice said, "You oughta treat that boy right, Shaw. If he hadn't knocked that knife out of Stegall's hand, you might not be here now. That pinhooker weren't piddling, he was going for your jugular, sure."

"That's right. You saw how all the others dodged back. Your boy's got a level head."

"Your boy's got grit."

"Goddammit." Clint thrust a bill toward Joedel without looking at him, then drew it back when he saw that it was ten dollars. "I've not got any change."

The waitress was fumbling in her pocketbook. "Here's three dollars, sonny."

The boy shook his head stubbornly, giving her a look of undisguised resentment. He would not touch her money.

Then his father snatched the money from her hands,

counted it, and held it out. "I'll settle with you directly," he told the woman.

"Here, Joedel. By damn, you can take this or leave it. Three dollars ought to buy your infernal mitt."

Sarah Thelma said, "Don't be so tight, Clinton. You use to be a big spender. You've not let the depression turn you to a tightwad, I hope."

Clint Shaw looked at her steadily. Then he handed Kirk Wiles the new ten-dollar bill. "I'll take a jar of that moonshine, Kirk. Let's all have another drink."

When Joedel left, his father was telling the others how when he was a boy he never had twenty-five cents, let alone three dollars, all his own at one time.

After watering the mules, the boy clutched the money in his right hand, walking rapidly up the littered ramp of the New Deal Warehouse. He did not experience the sense of triumph he had counted on. At the far side of the floor he caught sight of Trudy. She sat stiffly on a big rounded pile of tobacco, her head bent as the exhausted buyers slowly approached her on the last row.

His resentment of the waitress now encompassed Trudy. He did not feel sorry for her embarrassment. Instead, he felt only an undeniable urge to be rid of the money that came from the big-bosomed woman, just as he had spurned the piece of pie.

Turning away from the humiliated girl, Joedel found himself looking into the face of the blind guitar player. Behind the beggar stood his son, a boy no taller than the water boy on the chain gang. Joedel stopped and the boy nodded.

In the hustle and noise of opening day the Negro beggar was almost completely ignored. He sat in a cane-bottom chair against the hot tin wall. Joedel noted the cup wired on the neck of his scarred guitar. Except for a few pennies and nickels it was empty.

Although he could barely be heard above the noise of the wagons and trucks and the auctioneer's chant, the Negro was playing, his fingers moving rapidly over the frets. His nearly bald head was held at an angle and he seemed to be looking at the boy, his thick lips moving, sweat running down his flat black face. Although his eyes were milky, Joedel felt as though they bored into him. More, it seemed as if he were being sucked into the deep-set eyes of the folk singer, whose face was like a dark prophet's.

Now the beggar was singing, barely moving his lips, his voice low and gritty:

"This here's a needy time,
Yeah, this here's a needy time.
Singin' O Lord, give me one dime today,
I been in the storm so long."

Joedel recognized the song as one Shadrach Gillings sang sometimes in the fields, reverting to his geechee dialect.

"Just look what shape I'm in,
Just look what shape I'm in,
Cryin' O Lord, give me more time to pray,
I been in the storm too long."

Suddenly Joedel stepped toward the singing Negro. Quickly he dropped one of the bills into the blind man's cup. Then, wheeling, he ran down the front ramp, without looking at the surprised son.

"I'm much oblige to you, suh," the blind man called after him. "God bless you, suh."

There was not enough money left for the baseball mitt, but Joedel was inexpressibly glad.

ONCE ON THE CROWDED SIDEWALK JOEDEL HEADED
directly toward the dime store. He no longer thought of the
baseball mitt, but there was money enough left to buy gifts for
Sissie and Maddie.

He felt uneasy in the bright dime store. He had never
entered it before, although the school bus passed it so he knew
it was next to McDougald's General Store, down from the New
Deal Warehouse. It was not at all like Mr. Sam's store; there
was a different smell. He missed the familiar cobwebs and the
rust-spotted silver cash register and the jar of pickled pigs' feet.

His shoulders itched as he walked between the bolts of
cheap cloth and strong-smelling denim. He studiously kept his
eyes away from the pile of leather baseball gloves and tan
webbed mitts.

Joedel had not decided what to buy, and he hesitated
before a pile of lacy handkerchiefs.

The young girl behind the counter ignored him and he
did not venture to call attention to himself. She was talking
animatedly to two youths who wore caps at jaunty angles.

"I never promised him any such thing," she said. "I declare——"

"That's not what Myrtle said. She insinuated——"

"My stars above. What does she take me for?"

"I knew it was a fib all along."

"And I never cared no more for him than——" she hesitated, then nodded unmistakably toward Joedel.

The boy blushed scarlet and the two young men laughed uproariously. "I reckon not," one exclaimed. "The whole thing was a big story from start to finish."

Then she was standing before him in her shimmery white dress, her left hand patting at blonde shoulder-length curls. She glanced back at the grinning youths, and her full lips looked as if she had eaten a dill pickle.

Joedel lowered his eyes in confusion. He could think of nothing except how soft and white her hands looked. A lady's hands, not like his mother's rough field-browned arms. He reddened again, thinking of the picture of Jean Harlow above his cot.

"I said can I do anything for you?"

"Yeah, boy," one of the youths drawled. "Get the wax out of your ears and your eyes off her boobies."

"You, Horace!"

As she whirled around the wave of her perfume reached Joedel's nostrils.

"Yes, ma'am," he mumbled helplessly. "I'd like a bottle of that perfume yonder." It was reddish in a bottle with a fancy glass stopper.

Then he pointed to a length of red ribbon and one of the lace-edged handkerchiefs for Sissie.

The salesgirl pulled her lips down at her admirers, and he saw her shape the word, "tacky."

Joedel thought, They think I'm colored. But it did not matter, for now that he had settled on the gifts, he was unspeakably relieved. He felt as though an unsurmountable problem had been solved. There was enough money left to buy a small box of crayons for Sissie and a Big Little Book for himself. The change that was left would go into his secret Prince Albert can.

He did not even mind the giggles from the young men as he paid the peevish girl. Joedel grasped the brown paper sack firmly in his hands. There was a smile on his face as he strode back up the aisle, past the stack of baseball gloves. Already he saw the joy on the faces of his mother and Sissie when they opened up their presents in the lamplight.

As Joedel walked down the riverbank beside the New Deal Warehouse, he saw that his classmates had quit fishing. The auction was over and Clayton was becoming quieter. Occasionally there was the roar of the big company trucks taking the sheeted tobacco to the storage houses, or incoming loads to get ready for tomorrow's sales. But the heated frenzy of opening day was over; the rhythm of the town had changed, the tempo of traffic and men grew more subdued. Soon the men selling peaches and watermelons from open trucks would leave for the night.

As he cut across the washboard road toward the wagon, a black truck was pulling out of the parking lot. It stopped abruptly beside him, and Joedel saw, too late, that the driver was Mr. Baldwin, his daughter looking disconsolate beside him in the cab.

"You, boy."

Mr. Baldwin looked down at him, his hairy arm vibrating on the window. With his free hand, Joedel swept his coarse hair back, and stopped. The bald farmer seemed friendly, but the corners of Trudy's wide mouth were pulled down. In the rear of the truck a half-dozen Negro workers looked at him, grinning and talking quietly among themselves.

"Daddy——"

"You keep still now, gal."

Mr. Baldwin was smiling, his eyes squinched in the sunlight. "I reckon that was your dad that caught Stegall in there today. It took a man to do what he did, and I don't deny it."

Joedel nodded, swallowing.

"I inquired around after that fight and I learned sure enough, like Trudy claimed, you ain't a conk-haired nigger."

The voices behind the cab grew hushed, the black faces stiffened.

Mr. Baldwin was no longer smiling and his voice was raspy above the idling motor. "But it don't matter a good goddam to me, nigger or no. I'm not having any brass-ankle bastard smelling around my daughters!"

Joedel hardly heard what the red-faced man said, for he saw the tears spring into Trudy's eyes, her mouth forming words he could not make out. Beside her father she was gesturing, trying desperately to tell him something.

"You've done been warned, young buck."

Then Mr. Baldwin raced the motor angrily, ground the gears, leaving Joedel bewildered and motionless in a cloud of settling dust. He felt sorry for Trudy, and he regretted his resentment when he had seen her sitting dejectedly on her father's pile of tobacco.

"There you are, Joedel."

It was Booster, waving at him from Mr. Eller's wagon. He was sitting patiently on the tailgate. When Joedel asked if he'd heard any news of Cap'n Jim, he shook his dark head no.

"Papa and Uncle Ander and them others went over to that doctor's office to see. They ain't come back yet. I reckon they doing their trading. Papa made me stay to mind these mules and wagon."

Then Booster handed Joedel a piece of paper out of his bib pocket, smiling. "That young girl told me to give this to you particular."

Joedel had started to inquire about his father, but he took the letter. Immediately he became shy under Booster's knowing eyes. He waited until he was in the shade by the mule's head, before he read the penciled note:

Dear Joe Dell,

I've never been so mortified and put out with Daddy in my whole life. I explained all about how you were part Croatan and about the smartest boy in our class. But it didn't do a bit of good. He's still so provoked you'd think we did something awful there at the cotton gin.

I certainly intend to give him a piece of my mind but will wait until later. He's upset partly because the auction prices are so low, which does seem a shame.

Anyway, I want to ask you to come to our house next Saturday. Fanny Lee is giving a party, and Daddy won't be there.

Your friend,
Trudy

P.S. I will write you a letter and explain everything.

P.P.S. I'm sorry I never got the chance to tell you I enjoyed the peanuts and being with you. And I'm glad you had such a good sale. How does it feel to be rich?

Joedel folded the paper and put it in his pocket. That's what she was trying to tell me in the truck, he thought, about this letter. But one thing was sure: he wouldn't go to any party while Mr. Jim Eller was in the hospital.

The white mule beside him stamped impatiently, and Joedel ran his hand over her flank, speaking gently.

When he asked Booster if he had seen Clint, the dark boy looked at him curiously, his broad smile vanished.

"I seen him a while ago." He paused, nodding. "He stepped up yonder to one of them houses."

Booster hesitated when Joedel asked which one. "He said you's to wait for him here. He said it particular."

Finally, Booster admitted that he had seen Clint and the waitress go in the last house on the block. Joedel began walking away from the warehouse, the package tucked under his arm.

The Negro boy called after him. "You best stay here with me like your papa say."

It was the house opposite the cotton gin by the river, where he and Trudy had eaten the peanuts. A sign nailed to a maple said roomers were wanted. Momentarily Joedel paused under the tree, staring at the scaling banisters, the uneven steps with greenish dirt under them. The yard was bare and dotted with little holes made by night crawlers.

Suddenly the boy walked quickly across the yard to the side room with drawn shades. The tan shade was torn and when he stood on tiptoe, making his sore legs ache sharply, he could see in.

Inside he saw his father with the dark-haired waitress. The woman wore only her sweaty slip and the boy saw how the flesh sagged on her left arm when she reached up to stroke his father's neck. They stood by a nightstand with a basin and pitcher on it. At one edge the boy saw the fruit jar of whiskey and some bills.

He heard the waitress's throaty laughter, and his eyes blurred. He let his trembling heels down and leaned against the rough weathered boarding until his cheek pained him. The image of the new bills on the washstand was burned in his mind and he thought of his mother at home in the hot packhouse sorting tobacco. What made his father do it?

"You got a right to celebrate, Clint," he heard Sarah Thelma say.

"Weren't that a sale, though? I cured that tobacco and there wan't a basket on the floor that brought as much. Scarcely half as much."

"I meant the way you handled that thieving pinhooker."

"That dirty crook. Didn't I solid hit him though? I didn't nail him good but once, but I felt it jar my arm clean up to here."

"Let me feel. I declare, you're as strong as a bear—or that Max Baer. I bet you don't know your own strength."

Then there were whispers that Joedel could not make out, and he heard the springs on the iron bed sag.

A man was walking by on the clay sidewalk and Joedel saw him stop and stare. Without thinking, he walked out of the empty yard.

Now his stiff legs moved of their own accord, the boy hurrying past the cotton gin. Then he climbed the steep embankment and began walking up the railroad tracks by the river. His mind was emptied and a peculiar numbness came over him. "It is four miles to Ellers Bend," he whispered.

JOEDEL WALKED RAPIDLY ALONG THE RAILROAD
tracks, his eyes down, the noisy, steamy town receding at his
back, his lean shadow stretching before him. His stride was
awkward, for his legs were not long enough to take the crossties
two at a time. Already his legs were getting stiff from the morning's two-mile run. He was grateful for the soreness, for it
helped push from his mind the image of his father and the waitress in the shabby room. Each time he stepped, the paper sack
clamped under his elbow rattled, and the cinders crunched
under his tennis shoes.

When he reached the town dump he saw that a group of
Negroes were picking around in the trash, avoiding the thick
smoke at the center. Beyond it, the evangelist's tent was up in
the pasture, sunbaked and empty, with the sides rolled up, the
folding chairs neatly aligned. The wilted pasture was deserted
except for two gaunt cows chewing their cuds.

Below him and close by, a white man on the edge of the
dump saw him, then swiftly clawed up the weedy embankment.
When Joedel looked up, the grimy man stood confronting him
just beyond the narrow trestle. He had risen from the ashen
jungle refuse, materializing like someone in a bad dream.

The boy stopped, the hair on his nape seeming to rise, one foot on the trestle sleeper.

"What you got in that sack, boy?" He was a stocky white man, middle-aged, his unruly hair gray-streaked and sooty. He wore filthy khaki trousers and a sweat shirt with something the color of vomit on the sleeve.

Joedel did not reply, but he recognized the stoop-shouldered man with the beady eyes and hawk nose. He was the tramp who had stolen their lunch bowl from the wagon. Suddenly he was angry, not merely because of the stolen food itself, but because of his father's meeting the waitress that resulted from the missing dinner. He thought of the care his mother had taken, of her tired swollen body. If they had not eaten in the café . . .

"What's in the bag, sonny?" The unshaven stranger spoke with a metallic accent.

The boy glanced off at the Negroes picking in the town dump, but they took no interest in the two figures facing one another on opposite sides of the trestle.

"I say, what's in the bag, buster?"

Joedel swallowed dryly. "I've got a book, if it's any of your business." His voice seemed louder than he intended. Below the trestle he heard the gurgling of water.

The man snorted, reaching out a grimy hand. "We'll see about that. I don't want to hurt you, boy, but I'm hungry."

Joedel stared at him coldly, "No, you're not."

"How come I'm not?"

"Because you stole our dinner back yonder at the warehouse."

The unwashed tramp made a face and walked forward slowly, one sleeper at a time. "Peas," he said. "Cold black-eyed peas and rice and fatback. We don't eat garbage like that where I come from, sport." He laughed shortly, showing his gums.

Joedel thought, Then you'd better go back where you came from, I reckon.

The stranger took another tentative step. "If you ain't

got nothing but a book in that bag, you can pass on this trestle. But I'd swear you're lying to me, boy. I sure don't like chaps who lie to their elders. If I had a son that behaved like that I'd wear him out. I'd beat his stern, that's what I'd do." He spat a stream of tobacco juice into the stagnant water under the trestle.

Joedel shifted the sack and reached into his right pocket. His fingers gripped the cold handle of the Barlow knife, trembling. Instantly he knew, if need be, he could use the knife on the tramp, just as his father had struck Burke Stegall, and with that realization he was suddenly calm.

"Jesus Christ!" the man cried. "This little snot's got a blade."

Under the trestle a man laughed. Leaning forward, Joedel saw a light-skinned Negro squatting by the creek bank. He was washing something in the dirty water, and the skin on his yellow palms was crinkled.

"You best leave that there buck be, Yank. Else he pop that blade in you for stealing his hoppin john." The mulatto was soft and effeminate, and he spoke sullenly, his lips pouting.

Yank stopped in his tracks, as if pondering what to do. "You keep still. I got us our grub, didn't I?"

"Suit yourself and bleed all over them damn cinders. I ain't puttin' myself out to help."

"That's right. You ain't putting yourself out for nothing." Then he confronted Joedel again. "I don't want any trouble, buster." Cocking his head, he looked at Joedel's stiff copper face intently, his eyes skimming the dark coarse hair. "What are you, boy, nohow? You a Ne-gro?" He pronounced the two syllables distinctly, with an effort.

Silence.

"You a Ne-gro?"

"It's none of your business what I am."

Joedel thought, Yes, I'm a Negro. It doesn't take a black skin to make a Negro. What it takes is the way I'm treated, me and Sissie and Mama, though he knew his mother would be outraged if she knew he thought such a thing.

Almost imperceptively, he nodded.

The man below said, sulking, "I done warned you, Yank."

The tramp gestured impatiently and spat into the stream, close to his partner.

"No, you're not. You're not a colored. You're an Indian."

Joedel did not answer. His calm fingers played over the cool knife handle in his pocket. It gave him an ineffable sense of power, knowing he could use the knife on the bearded tramp if he were driven to it. Moving his lips, he thanked Cap'n Jim for the gift of the Barlow.

The stranger smiled, seeming to relax. "Okay, Hiawatha. You're all right. Hiawatha's a ten-o'clock scholar with a armload of books on his way back to the wigwam. Let's see what you're reading nowadays, then you can pass over our trestle, boy. That black troll down there won't leap up here and eat you."

He took a confident step forward, holding out his hand.

Suddenly, Joedel turned and plunged over the rail and down the embankment. Leaping through a clump of goldenrod and the shallow creek, he ran wildly across the lower edge of the dump and into the pine saplings. Out of the corner of his eye he saw the trash pickers staring, openmouthed.

"Come back here, boy!" the white man yelled, running after him. "I wouldn't harm a hair on your head."

From under the trestle, Joedel heard the maniacal laughter of the sullen Negro.

For five minutes he ran through a thicket and then tall pines toward the swamp. He could hear the stumbling tramp behind him. Then he half leaped, half fell into an old tar kiln, panting. He squatted on the thick bed of pine needles, catching his breath, slapping at the gnats that gathered around a cut above his ankle.

When he could no longer hear the man thrashing through the undergrowth, he crept from his hiding place. He was lost now, but he walked quickly away toward the swamp, with the thinning sunlight behind him, the soiled package gripped under his arm.

When Hester's Mill whistle sounded, he got his bearings again. Deciding against the railroad tracks, he turned right toward the Wilmington highway, lengthening his confident stride. To break the silence he began whistling the song the blind beggar had sung in the warehouse.

AFTER JOEDEL CLIMBED THE HIGHWAY EMBANK-
ment, he started walking blindly, with the sun setting behind
him. He kept his eyes on his stiff-legged shadow in the wild
marigolds or on the white cement that marked the halfway
point to Ellers Bend. He was glad to see that the chain gang
had quit working and returned to Silver Lake. Clutching the
paper sack as if it were a talisman, he hurried without thinking,
his soggy tennis shoes squishing in the wilted grass, unaware of
the trickle of blood running from his cut ankle.

There was a fresh spurt of traffic on the highway now,
farmers returning from market, their trucks and trailers empty
except for grading sticks wrapped in sack sheets or ragged
quilts. But since he did not look up or wave, no one stopped to
offer him a ride. He stretched his stride to keep ahead of the
one-horse wagon rattling behind him.

He had not reached the bridge when the International
truck ground to a stop beside him.

"Get in," Clint said, his voice carefully controlled.

Joedel looked at the open truck body where Mr. Eller

had lain on the Star of Bethlehem quilt. A block of ice was melting and trickling over the side and there was more water running from a pasteboard box.

Without a word, he got in and shut the door. He held the package between his wet knees.

"I ought to beat your butt. I've a good mind to frail the tar out of you, causing all that worriation."

Joedel made no reply, and Clint Shaw ground the gears and jerked the old truck into motion.

"They're doing what they can for Cap'n Jim. They say he might get to be all right. It's another stroke."

Shad and Booster had left with the wagon, and Clint had driven the truck to the Queen City hospital.

"Where you been, Joedel? I've looked high and low for you, boy. You know better than to run off like that."

Clint Shaw studied his son's face, his right eye swollen from the pinhooker's blows.

Joedel swallowed and told how he'd waited, then started home up the Seaboard tracks, only to be chased through the thicket by the tramp who stole their dinner.

Clint slapped the wheel angrily. "By God, Slade'll hear of this. What's that sorry sheriff good for nohow? Setting on his lazy rump up yonder while pinhookers steal us blind and sorry tramps sneak around accosting folks." He seemed glad to find someone to focus his anger on.

As he cursed the sheriff, Clint Shaw drove on. He was awkward with the truck and twice ran off on the shoulder of the road, venting his wrath on imaginary reckless drivers who forced him nearly in the ditch.

He glanced at Joedel's wet jeans and tennis shoes.

"Your mama'll be worried." Then he added meaningfully, "She might not want you to come next market day."

Joedel rubbed at the drying mud from the abandoned tar kiln and did not answer. He pushed his trouser leg down over the bleeding cut.

"Some things women ought not know," Clint repeated

judiciously, "Yes, sir, there's some things women are better off not knowing. A fact."

He turned to study his son's hurt face in the evening light and Joedel caught the hot odor of corn whiskey again.

Now, he told himself. Now he's going to bring it up.

Clint Shaw swallowed, embarrassed, then launched into his scheme to deceive Maddie. He had lost a few dollars in the crap game, and it would be better if Maddie didn't find it out. "She's gonna have enough to worry about with Cap'n Jim at death's door yonder in Queen City."

Joedel remained silent.

His father had thought the elaborate plan through. They would tell her the buyers had found out that Joedel's tobacco was almost rotten and bid only two cents a pound. Clint had picked up a blank ticket and filled it out at the warehouse. Shad and Booster had been informed and were in on the plan, promising to cooperate.

Clint put his hand on Joedel's knee. "Some things women better off not to know, son."

The boy thought of how his father had said that once while he was dressing a rabbit with boils on it, cutting them away from the edible flesh.

"Am I right?"

"How come you don't change the ticket on that pile Mr. Barefoot bought? Mama wouldn't ever expect——"

"I thought of that the first thing. I would've, but they're going to write up that sale in the papers, even put it on the radio," his father said proudly. Thirty cents a pound had set a sales record for the depression years.

"All right." Joedel nodded, thinking, So I've won and lost at the same time and that's the way it's got to be. He recalled his dream again, the gold coins which turned to crumbly vanilla wafers.

He knew how the word of his defeat would pass over the community, spreading like fire through dry broom sedge. He could anticipate the ribbing at Mr. Sam's store on Saturday.

But he did not brace himself against it; it did not seem important any more. Besides, it was he who had knocked the knife
from Stegall's hand. They would have to acknowledge that
much. He whom they teased because he couldn't wring a pullet's neck. A heathen Indian who couldn't gut a squirrel.

Presently, Clint Shaw's mood changed. He stepped on
the accelerator and drove even more recklessly. He was overcome by a talkative mood, telling Joedel of the new tablecloth
he'd bought Maddie.

"I got us a bait of oysters and fish back there, a big shad.
You know how your mama's partial to shad, she's been craving
some shad roe ever since she got pregnant. And extra ice. We
gonna have us some ice tea with that fish. How's that suit you,
boy?"

Joedel nodded beside his father, clutching his presents
that now seemed puny.

"Well, I'm sure some kind of hungry. I tell you I've put
in a solid day's work, not to mention I was up all night curing
out that barn of tobacco."

Then he looked at Joedel's muddy shoes and pant legs.
"Son, you're muddy as a hog. You can't let Mama——"

Suddenly Clint Shaw pulled the truck up beyond the
second cement bridge and switched off the motor.

"Get out."

"What are you going to do?"

His father was already out and sliding easily down the
embankment toward the little creek. "We gonna take us a swim
and clean up before Mama asks us too many questions. We
can't cause her any worry, not with her fixing to have that
baby."

Joedel held back. "This here ice'll melt, Papa."

Clint said there was plenty of ice to last for tea.

"There'll be somebody fishing yonder in that hole."

His father was already taking off his sweaty shirt, walking into the mossy trees arching over the narrow stream.

"Ain't nobody here. This hole's been limed long ago. Not

just limed, but dynamited and seined, too. I bet there ain't a frog or eel left."

When Joedel walked up, a water snake slid off a log and swam toward a gothic stump, sending out ripples on both sides. A dragonfly darted up from the harmless snake.

As the boy undressed, he saw that his father had already stripped to his undershorts. Now he stepped out and stood naked on the cypress log. His knuckles were skinned raw, and there was dried blood near the army tattoo. He looked tired, drained of all energy.

The boy thought, He thinks to wash himself clean, then go home and that will make everything all right.

"It's cool," Clint said. "First time I been cool this entire hell-heated day."

The sun was setting now, wan light still filtering between the massive trees. Embarrassed, Joedel glanced at his father's naked body, his wide shoulders and the enlarged veins on his forearms. His chest and buttocks seemed unnaturally white below the sun-and-wind-burned face and neck. He flushed at the thought of the waitress and the rented room. How could his father do such a thing?

"Don't dawdle now. Somebody'll come along and steal your stuff." Clint slapped at a mosquito at his hairy crotch, then dived in. A kingfisher gave a startled cry and flapped up from the stream below them.

Joedel waited. He scraped the mud off his shoes, then dipped the legs of his pants in, roiling the water. He wrung the water out of his jeans and hung them on a cypress log. A silver gasoline tanker roared past on the highway, its tires singing. As if it were a signal, Joedel dived into the dark water, grateful for its coolness.

As he came up, his father splashed water in his face.

"Race you," Clint called, pushing away from the stump with his feet.

Joedel swam behind his father, watching his long arms slice the water, the drops glistening on his dark hair. He fell behind, then turned back toward the huge cypress stump. He dog-paddled around the stump twice, blowing water out of his mouth, waiting for Clint to swim back from the far end of the pond.

The boy turned over on his back and floated, listening to the water gurgling in his ears. He let his arms and tired legs stretch, relaxing in the buoyant swamp-tasting water. Moving only his fingers, he let himself drift toward the mouth of the creek. He kept his eyes open, looking up at the dripping moss and stretches of darkening sky. A bat darted wildly over his head. Slowly the ache and tension drained out of him and Joedel felt that if he closed his eyes he might go to sleep, drifting down the creek and under the white bridge, perhaps as far as the Indian mound that was said to be lost in the deep woods.

Clint shouted. When Joedel turned over, his father was on the bank drying himself with his undershirt.

"We better make some tracks before Mama gets really worried."

Joedel walked toward his clothes, ashamed of the hairs at his crotch. As he began to dress himself hurriedly, he saw that the water snake had returned, its blunt head sending out quiet ripples toward the gothic stump.

A wagon was rattling past on the highway above them. Joedel buttoned his shirt, listening to the tired rhythm of the mule's hoofs.

CLINT SHAW PULLED THE TRUCK UP BESIDE THE peeling service pump and shut off the motor. Except for Mr. Sam's tabby tom, the porch was deserted and they saw at a glance that the store was closed. A cardboard sign that said "Closed. Gone Fishing" was stuck to the rusty screen with a staple.

For a moment father and son sat wordless in the cab.

"Maybe he's gone fishing like it says," Joedel whispered.

"Not likely. I'll go in and see if he's got word of the Cap'n from Queen City. He might've heard something on that there phone."

"Here then." Joedel held out a fifty-cent piece. "You give Mr. Sam this for me."

Clint Shaw looked at the coin, puzzled. "What's that for?"

"The bet. This morning he bet me them buyers wouldn't find it out. He said the snuff wouldn't cost me——"

"Hell, keep it. Maybe he was only joking." Then his father relented, pushing the coin away. "I'll take care of that for you."

Joedel watched him walk up the front steps. Clint Shaw
stood straight now, his hair still wet. He lifted his worn brogans
and set them down carefully, with strained dignity, smoothing
down his blue jumper.

Pausing by the kerosene drum, he looked through the
barred windows. "Mr. Sam," he called quietly.

The cat leaped from the porch and disappeared between
a stack of drink crates.

For what seemed a long time, Joedel heard nothing. His
father looked toward the little ferry in the middle of the muddy
river, his fingers drumming on the shaling pillars.

No news is good news, Joedel told himself. He had heard
his adult kin say that more than once. All the same, he felt his
muscles gathering tighter, like a guitar string being tuned.

Then a light went on. The boy thought, He's in there all
right. Mr. Sam's in there, and he's drinking from a fruit jar.

The door opened and his father was stepping inside,
catching the screen behind him with his left hand.

Joedel slid across the seat, but he couldn't make out the
mumble of muted voices inside. For a moment he debated
about going in himself to speak to Mr. Sam but decided against
it. He knew he would not be able to keep his lips from trembling. In his pocket he felt the bone-handled knife Mr. Eller
had given him the day of the hailstorm. Without thinking, he
began rubbing his finger over the smooth handle, pressing it
until it made his thigh ache.

"Dear Jesus," he said aloud, stroking the knife. Then he
sat hunched motionless for a long while, aware only of the yellow river flowing toward the sea and the broken spring under
him.

Presently, he saw Mr. Sam in the barred window, the
post-office window. The light was dim, and he could tell nothing from the blurred face and sloping shoulders.

The boy raised his hand, and the storekeeper nodded his
gray head, then turned away. His right arm seemed to fall in a

hopeless gesture, like the sleeve of a scarecrow when the wind dies.

"Dear Heavenly Father," he began to pray, closing his eyes.

But he could not keep still in the cab. Opening the door, he got out. In the failing light, Ellers Bend seemed changed, grayer. The houses seemed to huddle closer together under the huge mossy oaks. The boarded-up windows of the store across from Mr. Sam's seemed pathetic, like the blind Negro singer in the tumultuous warehouse.

To ease his mind Joedel turned away from the weathered frame houses, walking to the mill yard next to the store. He had liked the little mill, especially the smell of fresh sawdust and the snarl of the razor-toothed blade biting into the pine logs. Sometimes when the spinning teeth hit a knot, the saw screamed like a banshee, the spurt of sawdust diminished, until the leather-gloved sawyer pulled the lever and backed off. Best of all, he liked to climb the church-high sawdust pile and slide down on a rough slab. At the peak was a wooden cross, and he and Sissie had once raced up the orange mountain, stopping at the top to empty their shoes.

Now he looked up at the warped cross. When he blinked his eyes, it seemed to move, blurring. He walked back to wait in the truck.

Suddenly his father was opening the truck door, his face bleak in the waning light. "Move over," he said brusquely. Once again there was the strong odor of raw whiskey on his breath, filling the cab.

Joedel slid across the broken springs of the rough seat. He did not risk asking the question he wanted answered, but as he moved his stiff legs he caught sight of Mr. Jim Eller's snuff stains on the right window. They looked like dried blood, and he thought, There's my sign.

On the narrow ferry he did not get out of the cab as usual.

The humped-backed ferryman studied their grim faces, puzzled. "I hope ya'll had a good sale yonder at that auction."

Clint nodded curtly. "We had us a fine sale, thank you."

The ferryman turned away, straining at the cable, inching the ferry toward the north bank.

Turning to face Clint Shaw, Joedel saw his father's stiff lips. "The Cap'n is dead," he said. "He never come to, like they said he did. That stroke just naturally carried him off."

The boy gripped the bone-handled knife, gouging it in his flesh until his right thigh had no feeling. He was glad for the falling darkness, because his father could not see his quivering lips.

"He never suffered none. Mr. Sam said he never suffered the least bit. The best way to go. Mr. Sam never seemed tore up about it. Fact is, he expected it. I reckon we all did."

Toward the fertilizer plant a lone egret rose, slanting up from a tall cypress. It veered off downriver, flying with white grace. The boy watched it rise in the darkness until his eyes shimmered, and the beautiful bird was swallowed by darkness.

His father said, "I just remember. We clean forgot his plow sweep yonder at the blacksmith's."

Joedel thought of the forgotten ointment for Aunt Mary Mape's eyes, but he did not mention it.

At the bridge by the old mill race Clint pulled the truck over and stopped, idling the motor. At first Joedel did not know why. Glancing at Clint in the darkness, he saw his face was like a fist.

"You've not forgot that trout?"

It had been completely erased from his mind by the events of the day. But feeling a sudden elation, Joedel slid out of the truck and half stumbled down the winding fisherman's path, then under the black pilings. Squatting by the hairy root, he pulled at the short length of twine, mosquitoes whining at his ear, his nostrils filled with the heavy scent of the stagnant water. He felt the huge trout tug against his pull, surfacing weakly. Twisting the twine around one arm, he pulled steadily until the trout emerged from the dark water. Then he was holding the beautiful fish in both hands, its silvery tail splashing water against his aching chest. Smiling, the boy hugged the fish, thankful for its strength.

"Make haste now," his father called from the cab.

Quickly Joedel cut the string that bit cruelly into the huge trout's gills. Kneeling, he lowered it into a deeper place and shoved it away. For a moment the freed fish only floated at a sickening angle, then swerved sharply into the bank. Joedel watched the fish get his bearings, then streak for the deep waters. He wiped the slime off on his jeans, smiling.

"He broke the string," he told his father.

Clint put the truck in gear and raced the motor, crossing the wooden bridge with a sound like thunder.

"We got us plenty fish," he said. Then he added, frowning, "Some nigger stole it, more than likely."

Joedel started to tell the truth, but he could not explain, even to himself, why he had set the trout free. He remained silent beside his father, still holding the wet knife that Cap'n Jim had given him.

At the little Pentecostal church, Clint glanced at the graveyard, the roar of the truck echoing back from the tall pines.

"One good thing," he began, "one good thing come of the Cap'n's dying like that." He found it easier to speak once he had started and the boy listened, attentive.

"That sawmill back there. Mr. Sam told me he's going to start it up again and give me a job this winter in the yard, if I want it. Said him and Mr. Jim took out policies on each other way back yonder, and he's going to get that mill running with the money that's coming to him. It won't pay at first. There ain't nobody much that can buy lumber yet. But Mr. Sam says he's got that much confidence in President Roosevelt up there in Washington. At least, some folks around here will have jobs, and the lumber will be there when they can afford it."

Clint squeezed Joedel's leg, smiling. "If I get that cash

job for the winter, maybe Mama won't be always after us to go back to Badgerville. How about that now?"

"That'll be one good thing, Papa."

But Joedel knew the mill job was only an excuse his father could use against his mother's arguments for leaving Ellers Bend. No matter what, he knew that he would never return or live anywhere near Maddie's Indian kin. Without ever bringing it out in the open, Clint made clear his intention to stay away from Pembroke and all that it implied. It explained, in part, his fanatical drive to own the piece of land.

Now Joedel recalled what his father had said that winter while they were cutting wood to haul to Clayton. "You're not a Indian, boy, and I ain't raising you up to be one. Your mama ain't even a full-blooded Croatan, though she makes out like she is and is prideful about it. Hell, I'll bet she doesn't know two Indian words, let alone a dance or anything like that."

Joedel looked puzzled and remained silent. Clint wet the crosscut saw with kerosene and continued. "It's not that I don't care for her people. It's—it's just that in our day and time a Indian doesn't stand a chance, not in our part of the world."

In the cold air, his father's words had seemed to give off puffs of steam.

IT WAS FULL DARK WHEN HIS FATHER DROVE THE
truck up the bumpy wagon road and parked under the chinaberry tree. The chickens had gone to roost, and the hound was
not in sight. Clint switched the lights off, and Joedel saw the
soft lamplight in the kitchen window throwing a rectangular
glow across the yard. All around them they heard the familiar
chirr of insects.

Clint grinned nervously. "They got the dog locked in
with 'em. Scared of the boogers, I reckon." Then he added,
"After what happened today, I don't guess we have to worry
about folks in Ellers Bend. Not after I—not after we caught one
of the sorry rogues that's been stealing from them all these
years."

They were met on the porch by Maddie and Sissie, the
jubilant hound leaping up to greet them.

Maddie held the lamp and fussed at the dog. "Get down,
dog, I declare to goodness." She looked at Mr. Eller's truck,
then at her husband's swollen eye, puzzled.

Joedel realized that Shadrach had not brought her the
bad news but had driven the wagon to the Big House and

177

turned the mules out to pasture so they could walk home down the lane by themselves.

In the kitchen, Clint and Joedel distributed the presents awkwardly. Sissie squealed with joy at her ribbon and crayons, and Maddie flushed when she saw the perfume and handkerchief and the new tablecloth Clint had bought.

"Why, you've spent up the whole barn." She ran her hand over the smelly oilcloth and then she sniffed at the perfume. "You both have lost all your gumption." Her eyes sparkled in the lamplight.

"No, we've not, old lady. We've had us a sale yonder today, me and Joedel." Clint was fishing the sales tickets out of his jumper pocket. "We had a sale that putt the rest of the croppers in the shade. Old Shadrach was too shamed to bring my mules to the house."

Sissie asked, "You never stumped your toe on the railroad track this time, did you, Joedel?"

Clint broke in to tell how their dinner had been stolen by some no-count tramp and they were forced to eat at the café. "A waste in this world, and your good bowl gone, too."

"Merciful heavens!"

Joedel saw his mother's gray eyes on him, and he looked away at the knotted ribbon in Sissie's tar-black hair.

"What about Joedel's little basket?"

The room was filled with a sudden hush, and they heard a car blowing at Ellers Bend for the ferry. Clint looked at his son, and Joedel wet his lips.

"What happened, Joedel?"

He stared at the lamp. "They found it out." His voice was almost a whisper. "They went past it first, but a pinhooker smelled the rot and called the buyers back."

"Yeah, a crooked speculator bought it for two cents a pound. What I predicted all along. It scarcely paid the warehouse charges."

"I reckon what we did was wrong," Maddie said. "I wish now we'd marked it damaged."

"Water under the dam," his father said.

Clint Shaw's shoulders relaxed, and he began spreading the sales slips on the new cloth on the kitchen table, slapping them down as if they were aces and kings.

Sissie said, "I fed Coonie for you, Joedel."

"Never you mind about that little pile of rotten leaf. I tell you we had us a sale yonder today. That good grade more than made up for Joedel's rotten little mess."

His mother ran her hand over his head, brushing his damp hair back, "I'm sorry, son. Maybe Mr. Eller will give you another basket, maybe some old tips that cure out trashy."

"I'll go get your quilts, Mama."

His mother called after him. "I've already milked, son, and fed them mules."

The hound followed him out into the yard. The water was running off the truck body as Joedel pushed the beveled sticks aside, gathering up the Star of Bethlehem quilt. For a moment he let his hand rest where Mr. Jim Eller had lain on the ragged quilt. Looking up at the stars, he felt the resentment at the forced lie draining out of his tired body.

He had won and lost at the tobacco auction. Now the lie he told seemed fitting, for the whole plan had been a falsehood from start to finish. It had been a rotten scheme to outwit the buyers with a pile of tainted tobacco, and they were all caught in a net of guilt—his mother and father, as well as himself. And Mr. Sam because he had sold him the snuff on credit, knowing he was using it to disguise the damaged leaves, then made a bet to further implicate himself. Even Cap'n Jim, who had made the gift at the beginning, who knew and conspired with him to trick the buyers. Maybe his death was only one link in the chain that began with the storm-wet leaves.

At any rate, the boy agreed that there was an unimpeachable rightness in his wrongful gains being taken away from him by a toss of his father's dice. It was the other wrong he could not accept, would not forgive his father for. He would keep silent about it, as he would about the forged sales slip, but he could not forget.

Joedel waited until Clint had time to finish telling the

tale of the fight with Burke Stegall, and Maddie had washed around his swollen eye with kerosene. Then he walked with the bundle of quilts into his dark room. He dropped them in the corner where his tobacco had been piled that morning, the odor still faint in the room. He was waiting for Clint to break the final news.

"We sorted and tied near twice what you and Joedel laid out for us to get in order," Maddie said.

"No you didn't."

"Yes, we did. And Sissie was smart as a briar. She took off all those sticks by herself, Clint. I'm right proud of Sissie. She deserves a play-pretty."

"I took off all that baccer, Papa. Mama never helped none."

"Wednesday we'll finish that curing, Lord willing," Maddie said. At this rate, she added, they would have time to grade and tie three or four extra barns for Mr. Eller.

"No we won't." Clint's voice became husky.

"Why?"

"Mr. Eller's dead."

"No! He's not!"

The boy heard a bug beating against the windowpane.

"He is, Maddie. He's dead, all right."

"I declare! I thought something. You all didn't come and didn't come, and that owl last night . . ."

Joedel stood leaning against the rough door frame, thinking, I will remember this all the days of my life, this hour, this very second. His hand memorized the texture of the door-jamb as the boy looked at his father and mother in the lamplight in the little kitchen, smelling now of new oilcloth and kerosene.

Clinton Shaw's field-tanned face was serious, his damp shaggy hair sticking out in the back over his soiled collar. He leaned across the flowery oilcloth, his right hand out. His knuckles were skinned and his right eye was swollen nearly closed.

"Mr. Eller's dead, Mama."

He did not say the Cap'n or even Mr. Jim, thought Joedel. You cannot carve "the little Cap'n" on a tombstone and put that in a graveyard.

The proper name spoken by his father gave a sense of finality to Mr. Eller's death. It somehow made it irrevocable, underscoring the burgeoning sense of loss, adding to the growing tightness in his chest.

"Lord have mercy," his mother said, her hand curling back upon itself. Her fingers were like the brown tails of crawfishes, frightened.

Her eyes coated with wetness, and she turned to the boy in the doorway. Joedel's eyes met hers, and he let the tears flow unashamedly. His lower lip trembled, and it was as though a fine spray of salt was stinging in both his nostrils.

"I'm sorry as I can be," Maddie said. "He was a good man. He was the best friend Joedel—we had. It's a terrible shame."

"No. It's not," Clint said.

His mother's eyes widened. "Whatever on earth, Clint! What do you mean?"

"It's not a shame at all. Best way to die. If you got to go, it's the way I'd want to go myself."

"That's true, Lord."

Clint said that Mister Jim had died happy, the way he had wanted to die, with his boots on, so to speak. He was an old man, almost eighty, and he died at the market on opening day, doing what he enjoyed doing better than anything else. Besides, he wasn't afraid to die. "If he'd been afraid, wouldn't he have paid heed to the doctors and kept still and not been working and facing excitement and all? No, sir. The only thing he was afraid of was getting down bad sick and having one of his citified daughters tend to him. He as much as told me so himself."

Joedel thought of the sharp-faced, high-strung daughters who would soon arrive to take charge of the Big House. He retreated into his room, bent over and rubbed his face into the gritty sheet, feeling the ache in the calves of his legs.

He heard his mother say, "And that poor soul in the hospital at Raleigh. What on earth will she do now?"

"She's not to be told. It wouldn't do a bit of good, and she couldn't take it in anyhow."

"She's still his wife and she ought to know."

"Well, Mr. Sam said she wasn't to be told."

When he crept back to the kitchen door, his father was seated at the table, both hands on the oilcloth. Across the lamp he looked at Maddie's bereft face. Sissie walked around the table, prissing, with the ribbon in her hair.

They had done all they could for the Cap'n, his father was saying. No one could be faulted in that line. It just so happened that Doctor Clay had six baskets of tobacco on the floor at the New Deal Warehouse and they'd fetched him at once. Mr. Barefoot and the buyers had lifted Mr. Eller up and stretched him on Maddie's quilts on the truck body.

"I'm glad they were a comfort to him."

"Anyhow, he never let out a chirp, a word from the time he pitched over." Clint paused again. "Mama, I'll never forget it, if I live to be a hundred. The last words he spoke was, 'Look out for the knife, Clinton.' I hadn't noticed the switchblade, then Joedel lammed him with that stick, and the pinhooker dropped it, and I hit him good and hard alongside his jaw.

"Just then somebody yelled, 'Look to Mr. Eller!' There was a crowd pounding me on the back, and I couldn't break clear. When I saw him he was sprawled out, gray as a hornet's nest. Red Warner leaned over to him so fast he split the seat of his britches wide open."

Sissie giggled at that. "Did Joedel frop that old pinhooker, Papa?"

Clint grinned. "I mean to say he did. That boy can't gut a squirrel or wring a pullet's neck, but he putt a lump on that sorry scoundrel he'll bear to his grave."

His mother said, "Sometimes you have to be hard, son. You've got a right to be proud."

"They say his eyes were open and he sort of smiled. I didn't see it myself, but others did. Shadrach for one. They all swear he sort of smiled. You know that little smile of his'n."

Clint paused for the image of the smiling man on the quilt to soak in. Then he was telling how they'd rushed the Cap'n to the Queen City hospital, and how Mr. Sam had got the word over the phone that he was gone, no, dead. They had had a drink together, and the storekeeper asked Clint to be a pallbearer. Mr. Sam was to take charge of the funeral arrangements.

His mother smiled and brushed away the tears, her hands fluttery in the warm lamplight.

"Does this mean you won't get the chance to buy the land? It would be a pity."

"He said last week he'd get the papers fixed. I trust Mr. Jim. He's a man of his word, Mama. Mr. Sam was in on it, too. I know he'll look out for us. We can't start this year, with the estate tied up. It'll be next year." He paused. "Yes, it's the way it'll have to be."

Joedel stood in the doorway. He looked at his father's face and waited for him to say what he next spoke.

"But that don't matter now. Mr. Jim's dead, and it can wait, the land and all."

The words erased much, but not everything, Joedel thought. Not the throaty laughter of the fleshy woman in the slip and shoes with the red puffs. He had already forgiven the quick blow his father struck in anger.

"To be sure, it can. Tomorrow I'll fix some sweet potato pies to take to the Big House."

"Great God Almighty!" Clint said, standing up abruptly. "That reminds me. Did you all eat yet?"

"Sissie couldn't wait. We ate some warmed-overs."

"Old beans and Irish potatoes, Papa. I'm hungry again."

"Sissie, I'd purely be ashamed. You're not that famished."

"Fire up the stove, old lady."

There was a rush to get the packages on ice from the

truck. Clint made a great commotion, stomping on the porch, making a lot of noise, hugging the food close to his blue jumper.

He pulled the two little cans of oysters from the soggy bag as if it were a magician's trick.

Sissie's dark eyes widened.

"Let's us have a bellyful of oyster stew." He set the cans and box of crackers on the table. "I'm starved, Mama."

"Clint, you shouldn't've."

Joedel watched from the door as his mother's face burned with pleasure. Already she was firing the stove with red and white corncobs, then split pine. Her shoulders did not appear stooped and she moved with grace, in spite of the child she carried.

"And there's more, I tell you. Two big shad out there on ice—both of them wider than my two hands."

His father snatched up a gleaming knife and rushed outside to clean the fish on the chopping block.

"You shouldn't've done it, Clint," Maddie called. "You've got big notions for poor sharecroppers."

But he didn't answer. Joedel heard his father scaling and gutting the fish in the light from the kitchen window. He was fussing at the yellow tom, then singing under his breath. In the dark the boy could see the scales falling, cascading like a sharp-edged silvery rain.

He turned and stumbled toward his cot.

When the supper was ready, his mother called but Joedel did not answer. Stretched on his back in the dark room, he was staring at the ceiling.

"You, Joedel."

He could hear the chairs scraping and smell the sharp aroma of coffee and fried fish and fried corn sticks. He was hungry, but he would not eat with the rest. It did not seem right to gorge themselves with Mr. Jim's body not yet cold in Queen City.

Then his father was leaning over him, shaking his shoulder. "It's been a long hard day. You come on and eat now, boy." He leaned so close Joedel could smell the faint scent of whiskey on his breath, and he seemed to be staring into his hurt face.

"I'm not hungry, Papa."

He wished for his father to say that he had done a bad thing, then he would forgive him and get up and eat. But he wouldn't say it, and Joedel knew in his heart that he never would.

"You best come on and eat now," Clint said gruffly. "Tomorrow night we might go catting at that river, when we get through barning tobacco. You and me'll take Mama and Sissie."

Then he was gone.

When his mother came to tug on his arm, Joedel relented. He got up and let her lead him into the kitchen. He paused in the doorway, blinking. There were tears in his eyes that made the yellow light from the lamp shimmer, and the boy wiped at his nose with the back of his hand. Clint Shaw was turning up the wick until one tongue of flame licked the shade. He had taken off his shirt and was naked from the waist up.

The room was as hot as the New Deal Warehouse. Steam rose up from the bowls of soup, the platter of brown fish and crisp corn sticks.

There is something in this room, Joedel thought. More than the money his father had heaped in a little pile by the lamp in the center of the table with the fake sales slip. More than the bread and fish upon the table.

True, there was something in the room: a pulse, a force, which he could not put a name to. Not now, maybe years later, thinking of his father's huge hands, he could suggest a name for it, the force that translated green gummy leaves into dollars and that into meat on the table and flakes of light in his mother's gray eyes.

Joedel had never seen his mother's face so beautiful. There were tiny beads of sweat on her upper lip, and the roll of coarse hair at the nape of her neck had come unfastened and scraggled across one shoulder. She reminded him of the Indian maiden on the calendar at Mr. Sam's store.

"Son," his mother said, nodding at the soup at his place.

Joedel sat on the wooden bench. He took up the little crackers no bigger than swollen buttons and began crushing them in his soup. Soon he was eating with his family, spooning in the delicious hot soup, with Sissie slurping greedily beside him.

Later, from his little room, he heard Clint and his mother talking.

"Do you know Mr. Jim owned the first car there ever was in Ellers Bend? It's a fact. An old Chalmers, and the axles and transmission are up there this minute behind the stable, growed up in pokeweed. He wouldn't sell it for scrap iron this fellow's been buying up and shipping to Japan. He owned the first radio, too. Mr. Sam told me how the whole community— white folks—use to come to this very house to listen to 'Amos 'n' Andy.'" Clint paused. "Mr. Sam was telling me old-timey things like that. His mind seemed to go back yonder and dwell on them."

"Ain't that something now?"

His father spoke of Mr. Jim Eller's accomplishments as if they were somehow his own.

"Lord, won't there be a mess of people in that Presbyterian Church? And the flowers . . ."

"It won't hold them all," Clint said flatly. "It won't begin to hold everybody."

Undressed in bed, Joedel stretched his sore legs. A moth was beating its wings against the window. For a moment his mind was crowded with the faces of the day: the conniving pin-hooker, the evil man on the trestle, the blind Negro and Trudy's stricken face, the doctor kneeling on the truck body. But he refused to focus on them. He could not, even if he'd tried.

Instead, his mind plunged ahead to the funeral which would be held in two days, with his own father a pallbearer.

Maddie would brush Clint's dark suit, and he would wear it with his only Sunday hat. He had not worn it since Grandma Oxendine's funeral at Pembroke.

Tomorrow, before day, his mother would bake the sweet potato pies to be carried to the Big House, then they would all harvest another cropping of tobacco. For that would not wait for anything, lightning or death. Day and night the broad leaves were ripening, yellowing on the head-high stalks. They must be gathered, even if the owner himself lay in the silver-handled casket in the parlor of the Big House. It was a natural rhythm not to be altered or broken.

And since the heat would not be run up in the barn until Thursday, Joedel would go to the funeral, riding with Clint and the pallbearers, not far behind the long black hearse. His mother would stay to mind Sissie, but she could not go anyway, for her confinement was close at hand.

They would have to let the Negroes come to the Cap'n's funeral, his tenants, he thought. They would not come inside the crowded church. No, the Negro sharecroppers would stand on the sidewalk across the street in front of the soda shop or the little fish market. They would be dressed in their best clothes and holding their felt hats in strong hands: Shadrach, Doll Boney, Quince and Uncle Ander, the oldest, their children dressed in clean overalls or starched white dresses. Their dark faces would be somber in the sunlight, and they would listen to the hymns from the open stained-glass windows and never say a word among themselves. Later, without anyone speaking to them, they would be off to one side in the cemetery, staring at the open grave under the green canopy. Maybe their wives would join them, standing among the grave markers and skimpy broom sedge, just beyond the circle of grief.

Joedel would see them and be grateful for their presence.

He wished that it was to be a Negro funeral, so that he could stand up and speak a few words. That was why he liked their buryings. For a moment he thought of Ariel Lacey in the

clay ditch with his shoes untied. Then he recalled the last
Negro funeral that he had been to with Cap'n Jim. It was
Shad's oldest son, who had drowned in Millers Creek. Enoch
had been a good cropper and never slubbered any work that
came to his hand. But that didn't make an iota of difference, for
the Cap'n always went to the funerals of his sharecroppers,
sorry or good. He remembered how the dark mourners had hollered or moaned until it seemed the roof of the New Hope
Church would surely rise and sail away to Zion.

Joedel remembered how one young man, with his hat
on, stood up in the congregation and spoke a few words, beyond the singsongy preacher's, about the dead youth. He had
told simply what he best remembered about the deceased—in
this case it was the smile he always greeted the world with, in
hard times or good. Joedel liked that best of all the funeral,
even better than the jazzy piano and earnest singing.

He would like to do that for Cap'n Jim. He could picture
himself in the Clayton church, and he was standing up with all
eyes in the congregation on him, everybody craning their necks,
their funeral-parlor fans still all of a sudden. His hands were
resting on the polished pew in front of him, above the wooden
piece with the three holes in it to hold the Communion glasses.
What would he say?

Joedel spoke the words in the night: "I would like to say
that Cap'n Jim Eller was a friend to us all. He drove us hard,
but he never did ask of us what he wouldn't do himself. Here
was a good man, and we will never see his like again in this
world." He didn't know whether to say amen or not, but he said
it and sat down.

Anyway, they would have to let the Negroes come.

For a while he thought of the note Booster had given
him, and the letter yet to come. He hoped Trudy wouldn't do
anything silly, like putting the stamp on upside down. But no
matter what, he knew he was in for a lot of teasing from Mr.
Sam.

His father came to the doorway, his shoulders bent,

bone tired. For a moment he stood with the smoky lamp in his hand, looking at his son as if he intended to come in.

"You better get some sleep, son. We'll be up before day to take out that barn of tobacco and putt another one in."

The new curing would be stored in his bedroom and the cycle would begin again.

"All right, Papa."

The boy turned toward the wall, and the wick was blown out. The moonlight played over the immortal blonde goddess above him, her hair a golden halo, and above her, a mustached man in boots with a black armband, who raised one arm as if to claim the boy on the cot.

Joedel slept.